# THE BAYNES CLAN

# CALIFORNIA EAGLES

*Also by Barry McCord*
*in Large Print*

Wyoming Giant

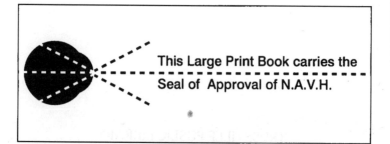

This Large Print Book carries the
Seal of Approval of N.A.V.H.

# THE BAYNES CLAN

# CALIFORNIA EAGLES

## John S. McCord

**Thorndike Press • Waterville, Maine**

Published in 2003 by arrangement with P.M.A. Literary and Film Management, Inc.

Wheeler Large Print Western Series.

The text of this Large Print edition is unabridged.
Other aspects of the book may vary from the original edition.

Set in 16 pt. Plantin by PerfecType.

Printed in the United States on permanent paper.

**Library of Congress Cataloging-in-Publication Data**

McCord, John S.
     California eagles / John S. McCord.
        p. cm. — (The Baynes Clan)
     ISBN 1-58724-309-1 (lg. print : sc : alk. paper)
     1. Baynes family (Fictitious characters) — Fiction.
2. California — Fiction.   3. Large type books.   I. Title.
PS3563.C34439 C35 2003
   813'.54—dc21
                                     2002028096

To Joan,
first to see, first to help,
and to Gary Goldstein,
editor and friend

# ONE

AMADOR COUNTY, CALIFORNIA
OCTOBER 28, 1870

Ward pulled his matched team of Morgan geldings to a stop on the crest of a small knoll and sprang to his feet. His voice came out strained. "Kit, look yonder. What do you think that might be?"

The former Kathleen Iris Thackery, now Mrs. Ward Silvana Baynes, stretched on the wagon seat, yawned out loud, and elbowed his leg. "Ward, you danced my feet off, and I'm too tired for any more of your devilment. Let's go. It's so dark out here nobody can see anything. Stop your foolishness and take me home."

"No, no, I'm not joking, honey. Look at that. It looks like some kind of big light."

"If you scare me again with one of your ghost tricks in the dark, I'll scream with all my might, Ward. It'll take you a mile to get the horses settled down again."

Ward dropped to the seat and flicked the reins. "Giddap! Giddap!" The hot-blooded team surged forward and brought a stifled scream from his startled wife as her head snapped back.

"Ward, be careful. You'll turn us over in the dark."

"No, I know this trail. I only saw a light like that two times before, Kit."

"When?"

"When I saw a barn burn far away in the night and when I rode in the dark toward a big town. Kit, I fear it's a fire, and it's out toward our place."

"Oh, no. Ward, don't tease me. Please." She sat up straight and stretched to see while she held on to the bouncing seat with both hands. "I don't see anything."

"I'm not teasing you, sweetheart. I'm scared. We'll see better when I get us to the top of that ridge ahead. My heart's thumping."

Pounding at a full gallop, the team crested the ridge, and Kit gave a forlorn little wail. "I see it now, Ward. It does look like a fire. Oh God, the baby!"

His words came out tight, like he was lifting something too heavy. "Now don't worry, honey. Maria and Rudi won't let anything happen to him." Ward's face twisted in the darkness as he silently cursed himself. Wobbly speech wouldn't help steady his woman.

He wanted to do better. A situation like this called for a man to be calm and strong, but he couldn't seem to catch his breath. His hands shook till he feared he'd lose the reins, so he rode with them clenched tightly in his fist. He leaned forward, trying to urge more speed from the team. He knew it made him look stupid with the horses already stretched out till their bellies almost touched the ground. To hell with it. Kit had seen him look stupid plenty of times before, and she still loved him.

She lifted one hand from its grasp on the seat and put it on his shoulder. She made simple moves in a way no other woman could match. Only Kit could send him a vote of trust, a loving gesture of her confidence in him, all without a word, just a light pressure on his shoulder.

Tears leaked from Ward's eyes and traced damp trails in the wind back into his sideburns. This was all his doing. He had talked her into leaving the baby at home. He recalled the points he had made, one by one. No need to take the little two-year-old toddler all those miles over a dusty, bumpy road to a dance. It was time for him to do without his mother for the first time. A few hours wouldn't hurt him, not even a whole day, for heaven's sake. The little fellow would have Maria's devoted attention every minute and be spoiled to death before they could get back home.

Spoiled to death? More likely burned to death. Ward shuddered and felt Kit's hand tighten on his shoulder. Her touch steadied him, and he felt his chest loosen. His breath slowed, and the urge to groan receded. He could feel himself draw strength from her. He knew he should be the strong shoulder for her to lean on — after all, he was the man. But often as not she was the one who gave him power when he felt down and weak. As long as he had her by his side, he never felt like a dropped egg for long.

The tears eased for a moment and he took a deep breath. Then the images of a little wide-eyed boy dancing with upheld arms came to him. The memory of wide blue eyes just like Kit's drove a spike deep into Ward's laboring chest. If anything happened to that baby, Ward knew he would drop in his tracks and die. He couldn't bear it. Nor could he survive the constant reproach in Kit's expression if something had happened. The idea to leave his son at home had come from him. Now it looked like that might have been the worst idea he'd ever had in a life full of mistakes.

Ward felt his heart in his throat. Everything inside him strained and tried to tear loose. Lather from the laboring horses sprinkled his face and he eased the pace. God help him, but he couldn't kill his horses. He might die in agony from unbearable grief and shame, but he would face his Master as Ward Baynes, a horseman. Some things lie too deep for a man to change though he could burst his heart in the effort.

Kit wiped his face with her handkerchief. "That's good. You have to slow them. We still have two or three miles to go. Killing them won't help us get there faster."

She could read his mind. Surely God could have made only one woman like her.

"It must be the house, Kit. I don't even have hay put up in the new barn yet."

His quick glance caught her shaking her head when she answered. "How could it be? I never saw a better double-wall chimney than we built. Could Maria have dropped a lamp? If she did . . . she wouldn't run out without the baby."

He tried a chuckle and almost made it sound right. "Of course not. She thinks she has a half interest in that boy. When he grows up, she'll be demanding half his stud fees."

The hand on his shoulder squeezed hard. "That's better. You sound like Kid Baynes again, the gunfighter I married. Remember him? The one who told jokes when a sane man would have been scared speechless. I think it's a dark streak that runs in your whole family." She kissed the side of his neck.

"No, Kit, not a dark streak. A dumb streak."

A wheel found a rock and threw her against him hard. She drew back, tucked her flaring skirt, and said, "Just remember where to find that one again."

He patted her knee and tried to smile. "Thank you, warrior wife. My hinges pulled loose for a minute. You put me back together. I'm ready to pretend I'm tough again."

"Oh, oh, oh." Her soft cry of despair came when they rounded the last bend and rode out of

11

the dense woods. Kit's moan and the light reflecting from her eyes made Ward turn to face a spectacle worse than any nightmare. Their beautiful house in the gentle, green valley of their dreams burned with eye-searing brilliance. A two-story-tall image of his hopes, the roof to cover the bed he'd planned to die in one day, born of two years' hard work and most of his money, went up in smoke.

Flames roared skyward in blasts and whips of huge blue, yellow, and orange pillars of destructive rage. Twisted streaks of sparks and glowing cinders spun and danced and lazily drifted like a reeling universe of wayward stars.

One wall groaned like a tortured creature and wavered, but it held for a second or two, like a brave man's spirit fighting a mortal wound. Then it sank slowly inward just in time to catch a fatal blow from a falling section of roof. The house expelled an enormous dragon's breath when the collapse of wall and roof spewed a tide of flame and cinders across the ground, a wickedly beautiful blanket of hellish jewels.

"Do you see Maria or Rudi?" Her hand left his shoulder, and she dropped to the ground.

The lathered, exhausted horses jerked in their traces and edged away from the fire. "Come back up here and hold these horses. I'll go see if I can find them."

"Tie them or just leave them, Ward. I'm going with you."

He jumped down. "You're right. They won't go

far, tired as they are. Let's go." He spoke too late. She had finished with waiting, her patience exhausted during the long ride. He had all he could do to catch up to her. Kit carried no extra weight on her small frame, and she ran like a startled fawn, low to the ground and sure of foot.

Then Ward noticed the barn. Because it lay beyond the house, he simply hadn't thought to look for it, hadn't had it long enough to get used to it being there. Its timbers had already fallen, but flames still rose high and wide. Thus perished a new barn, a barn too young to boast even a single gray board, too young to have sheltered its first newborn colt or filly.

"Stitch? Stitch, baby, where are you? Can you hear me?" Kit's voice was full of desperation.

Ward pulled her away from the burning house, and held her close for a moment. The hateful light let him see hair already singed above her brow. "Don't go so close, Kit. No point in it."

She looked up at him for a moment, eyes blank. Then she shook herself as if abruptly awakened and patted his chest. "I'm all right," she said. "I don't know where to look."

"I don't either. Let's just walk around the house. Maria and Rudi must be around somewhere. They'll see us in the light and give us a holler. Then we'll grab our little Stitch and hug him till he gets tired of it. He'll be with Maria and Rudi. He's got to be."

Kit jerked to a halt and pointed. "What's that?"

13

"Where?"

"There. Right there where I'm pointing."

Ward ran the last few steps to the dark lump on the ground, and he thought before he knelt that he had found Rudi. But he was wrong. Only Rudi's hat and favorite blanket in the flickering shadows. The half-Indian, half-Mexican man had an actor's gift. He could change a few items of clothing and become Indian, Mexican, or dark Anglo whenever it suited him. He wore these garments when he chose to be Mexican, usually when he planned another campaign to melt Maria's heart with his Latin charm.

Ward touched the tight weave of Rudi's Mexican poncho and straightened, forcing himself to scan the area in an orderly search. Nothing. Dread tightened his throat. If Rudi were close, and if he were able, he'd call out. Ward wouldn't need to search for him.

As if Ward's thought prompted the call, it came. *"Patrón. Aquí. Yo estoy aquí."* A flicker of movement drew Ward's eye to a clump of bushes. He couldn't hold himself to a walk. He ran to Rudi as fast as he could, but Kit still got to the downed man first.

She dropped to her knees beside him, and she already had a hand to his forehead when Ward approached. Her question came in a gentle murmur. "Oh, Rudi, you're hurt. What's happened?"

He raised his head to look only at Ward, as if something in him refused to see Kit. Even in the poor light, Ward saw a new Rudi, a man he'd never seen before. His rigid, stark expression would fit a raiding Comanche better than the savvy horse trainer Ward knew. He stared over Kit's shoulder straight into Ward's eyes, and he spoke in Spanish, a language he knew Kit understood only a little.

Ward caught the signal. Nothing subtle about it. Rudi barely stopped short of shoving Kit aside. The normally courtly horseman meant his remarks to be man to man. Kit, a woman, mattered not at all to him at this moment.

"I have failed you, *patrón*. I have lost my honor. You left me to defend your home, and I failed. Let me tell you of it. Then you have my permission to kill me."

Ward dropped to one knee. "Where is Stitch, *amigo?* Where is Maria?"

"Gone. Both of them. Carried away. Four men. Anglos." Rudi's head dropped back, and his gasping breath faltered.

Kit whispered, "He's shot through both legs. There's blood everywhere. I'm going to the wagon for my things." She sprang to her feet and vanished like a woodland sprite.

Hand on Rudi's shoulder while he waited for the man to gather strength to speak again, Ward fought a wild drive to shake the words out of him.

Kit, always quick to think and act, was bringing the wagon. Ward marveled at her. No screaming, hysterical mother with a lost child there. No, not Kit. A caring mother, always brave and

15

thoughtful, making herself useful, that was Kit's way. She never cried over spilt milk; she reached for a mop first and did her bawling later, if ever.

Rudi fixed his grim gaze on Ward again. "If you want the boy, they say for you to come to the desert. Bring ten thousand in gold. Come alone. If you don't come, they'll send you the boy's ears and leave the rest of him for the vultures."

"What desert?"

"They said for you come to Vallecito Stage Station. When they see you there, they'll tell you what to do next."

"My God, Rudi, that's almost all the way to Mexico."

Rudi nodded, and Ward guessed the man had little breath left.

"Was he hurt, *amigo?*"

"No. They took Maria to look after him. And for other reasons." The last remark thinned Rudi's lips and narrowed his eyes to slits.

"Our time will come, *amigo.* Tell me all you can."

Kit drew the wagon to a halt and sprang down holding her bag. She always carried her bag of necessaries when away from home, even for a short trip to town, just as the desert-trained Ward had carried his guns and canteen. Without a word, she started to work on Rudi's legs. Ward felt only a slight twitch when she lifted his coat and slipped his knife from its sheath at the small of his back. Rudi's eyes widened when she slit a trouser leg from hip to knee with one clean slash.

"Worry about your modesty after you recover from your wounds, *amigo.*" Facing Ward's hard grin, Rudi blinked rapidly but he made no protest. Ward gripped Rudi's shoulder. "Talk to me."

Rudi's eyes closed as if he couldn't bear the sight of the world and still say what he must. "My fault. I came up to the house. You were away so I thought I had a good chance to use my charm on Maria. You know I have come to desire her. She hates my pistol, makes me take it off when I come around to visit."

Kit said flatly, "Move, Ward. You're in the light."

Ward moved around to the other side of the stricken man. "Go ahead, Rudi. What then?"

"All I could see or hear or smell was Maria." He obviously felt Kit didn't understand his Spanish. He would never have used such explicit language if he thought she might understand it. His type of man would never mention the smell of a woman in the presence of another lady. Nor would he show fear. Some things a proper man could never do — never.

"They came from nowhere. I never saw them until too late. They didn't even speak, just shot me in the leg. When I didn't fall down right away, they laughed and shot the other leg. Maria screamed and picked up Stitch. She tried to run in the house with him, but they beat her to the door."

"Had you seen any of them before?"

"No, but they knew you, *patrón.* They came for

17

you. I hear them say your name many times. I hear one say, 'If we can't get Baynes, take the whelp. We'll make him come to us.' "

"Names, *amigo?* Did you hear any names?"

Rudi squeezed his eyes tight with his effort to remember. "I'm sorry, *patrón.* I think so, but I can't remember now. My life is leaking away into the ground under me."

Kit said, "I've stopped the bleeding, but he must be terribly weak. He needs a doctor. I can't even clean these wounds properly out here."

Ward stood and walked away a few steps, eyes scanning the ruins of more than three years of his life. The land remained, but his buildings and everything they contained still lighted the sky. He had a wagon and a team of tired horses. He didn't have a saddle. He didn't have an extra shirt. He didn't even have a blanket to wrap around Kit. None of it seemed to matter anymore.

First, he must try to save Rudi. No effort to trail the attackers made sense until morning light anyway. He'd best try to bring help here — a rough wagon ride would probably finish the wounded man. At least Rudi's own blanket would protect him from the night chill, and he probably needed it now. Ward turned to tell Kit, but she'd already covered him.

There was still Peepeye down in the little breeding shed in the woods. He'd never thought of it as a hiding place before, but maybe it had inadvertently served that purpose. Peepeye had a

18

wide streak of jealousy. The big stud put up a wicked fuss every time he saw Ward working with other horses. The inconvenience of isolating him from the bustle of other work might have turned into an actual blessing.

If he had an ounce of luck in a world suddenly gone sour, the raiders hadn't found Peepeye. He couldn't remember if he'd left a working saddle down there, but he'd at least have his racing saddle. Through God's grace, he'd put off moving Peepeye and most of the other gear from the little shed to the new barn. He could even offer Kit a blanket while he rode for help. It'd smell of horse, but she'd be warm, by heaven.

He didn't need to raise his voice. "Kit, I'm going to see if they found Peepeye."

"Wait a minute." She bent over to put her ear close to Rudi's mouth. When she straightened, she said, "Rudi says they didn't. Hurry."

Ward trotted away, too anxious to walk, feeling as if his heart pumped real blood for the first time since he'd seen the light in the sky. At least he was doing something now. He could face hunger, hardship, pain. None of that worried him anymore. Helplessness had nearly crushed him. Standing still while fear and his own imagination soured his stomach and dissolved his backbone, that defeated him.

Mounted on Peepeye, with Jesse in his holster and Nadine in her long saddle scabbard, he was a match for any man. Ward Baynes, the quiet family man known for his genius at breeding and training horses, would have to wait. Kid Baynes would rise again from the ruins and destruction of this day. Kid Baynes, the vicious, icy gunfighter, would be different this time from the fresh youth who had earned the nickname. The young Ward Baynes had killed efficiently and coldly, forced to, but so indifferent that other men thought him abnormal. This Kid Baynes, older and harder, would be different.

His stride lengthened and power seemed to flow like a warm torrent through him. The new Kid Baynes would feel joy, would scream his own exultant war cry over the bodies of the men who shot his hired hand, kidnapped his maid, burned his home, stole his son, grieved his blameless wife. A low cry came unbidden from his dry throat, a primitive groan of ferocious blood lust.

# TWO

Near Victoria, Texas
November 1, 1870

Milton Baynes enjoyed feeling so smug a lesser man would have suffocated from it.

Cris, his short, usually slim, red-headed wife, asked, "What are you smirking about?"

"You look like you swallowed a watermelon seed and let it get out of control."

She faked an accusing tone. "It's your fault I look like this."

"It better be my fault. And you can stop fishing for compliments. If you were plain, I could understand it, but why beautiful women always need compliments mystifies me." He patted her swollen middle. "I forget. How many did you say you got in there?"

"One. How many times are you going to ask that same dumb question?"

"Just checking. I keep thinking you've changed your mind. Look's like you've made room for about six. It's all right with me if you have a litter."

Her lip curled with mock disgust. "I don't think I'll ever understand what men think is amusing. Do you really think that remark is funny?"

"Yeah."

"Don't you think it might be just a little flippant and undignified to talk about your wife having a litter?"

"Yeah."

"Push."

Milt flexed a leg to put the swing into motion. She insisted that the chains be adjusted so the seat rode high enough to provide a comfortable level for his long legs. As a result, her feet didn't touch the porch floor. She preferred to sit with her feet tucked under her anyway, or in his lap. The chains suspending the swing from the roof of the porch made a pleasant squawk she seemed to like.

"You think the way I talk is undignified, woman?"

"Yes, and disrespectful."

"All right. You tell me about it. What's dignified about having a baby?" He spoke in a prissy, falsetto tone. "Seems like it's frightfully messy to me."

"Milt, you're about to make me mad."

"No, I'm not. I can tell when you're getting mad, and I get me some distance to avoid injury. Besides, I can see you grinning like an overfed kitten."

As if prompted by his comment, she smiled up at him. "You don't know a thing about having babies, so you can just shut your sassy mouth."

"Yes I do. I've been talking to the big boys. I found out what causes this kind of problem in the first place."

"Really? Now that's exciting news. What did the big boys tell you causes what you call a problem?" she asked.

"Watermelon seeds. Women got to be careful. If I was a woman, I'm not sure I'd eat watermelon at all."

"All right. If that's so, what prompted that remark about the fellow who caused my condition using up a lot of energy doing such a good job?"

"Did I say that?"

"Just a minute ago."

He shrugged. "I guess I was thinking about how I always try to pick the best watermelons I can find."

"Push."

He flexed a leg again. "How much longer are you going to take?"

"Probably two more weeks. Maybe a month. Getting impatient?"

"Yeah. The big boys tell me you got to finish with this one before I can get you started on another."

"Milt, that kind of talk is indelicate. You have no business saying such things to a woman in my condition."

"You don't make a man feel delicate. You make a man feel smug and chesty. I guess it's a burden you got to bear."

She flipped both hands in pretended disgust and changed the subject. "Did you make a list like I asked you to?"

"What list?"

"Names. Push."

He flexed a leg, and the swing moved gently. "Don't need a list. I've decided."

"No, you didn't. We're going to decide together."

"Not necessary for you to trouble your mind about it, woman. I'm the boss, so I'll make all the decisions. If it's a boy, we'll name him Sylvia. If it's a girl, we'll call her Henry."

"I guess this is one of those days when it's impossible to get you to talk seriously." She glanced over her shoulder and then turned to stare. "I see Uncle Caleb coming back from town. He's got somebody on the wagon with him and a rider alongside."

"Yeah." He stared straight ahead.

"Aren't you curious about who it is?"

"Naw. I already know."

"You do not. How could you know? You haven't even looked around. Who do you think it is?"

"That's Winston Mill, your dwarf brother riding alongside, and that's the almost brand-new Mrs. Winston Mill on the wagon with Uncle Caleb."

"Milt! You invited Win and Eva and you

didn't even tell me? I'll kill you. Nothing's ready. You make me so mad I could pinch your head off."

"Not me. Caleb invited them. Pinch *his* head off. I don't see why though. They're his guests. They'll stay with him over in that big house of his."

"Why didn't you tell me if you knew about it? This is awful. We're not ready to have them visit."

"I didn't want you fussing around wearing yourself out. Now Win and his woman will see the disgusting filth and revolting disorder we live in when we're not expecting company."

Her face twisted when she looked down at her shapeless dress and bare feet. Her hands rose to her hair for a second before covering her face. "I look terrible. I can't even run in the house to fix myself without looking like a fool. They're so close they'll see me."

Milt stretched out a long arm and pulled her hands away from her face. He leaned toward her and stared into her eyes. His face fixed in grim expression, he said, "Cris, it's too late. They're going to find out sooner or later anyway. Just relax and let it happen."

Her mouth was in an irritated straight line, as her eyes widened in alarm. "Find out what?"

"They're going to find out that you're the most beautiful creature in the world, natural, just like you are, neat, clean, and expecting. We'll have to make them swear to secrecy or artists will come from all over the world to paint you. They'll help

25

us keep the secret in the family if you're going to let it upset you so much."

He pulled her against him and put both arms around her. With her head on his chest, Cris said, "Push."

Milt flexed one leg and twisted to look over his shoulder at the rider who reined to a halt beside the porch. "Hello, brother-in-law. You come to visit your chubby sister?"

Winston Mill dismounted, stepped up on the porch, shook hands with Milt, and wiggled his rear into the narrow space left at the end of the swing. He pulled Cris away from Milt, wrapped his arms around her and crooned, "My poor sister. You look terrible. What has this lecherous man done to you?"

Cris giggled and said, "Push." Both men obediently flexed a leg and laughed at each other.

Caleb Cowan reined the team to a stop and helped Win's wife down from the wagon. "Got a telegram for you, Milt. Lucky thing for you I was in Victoria when it came in, so you got it hot off the wire." He stepped up on the porch and handed the yellow envelope to Milt. "I carried that thing all this way without reading it. I'm so overloaded with curiosity I think my milk's gone sour."

Win's wife rushed to Cris and bent to kiss her cheek. They exchanged smiles and murmured greetings. Holding hands, they turned to watch Milt, both failing to conceal concern.

Milt tore open the envelope and glanced at the message. Blunt, cruel words met his eyes. He blinked and read them again, hoping he'd mis-taken their meaning. One quivering breath was all he could manage before the dismal hope of error vanished. His face must have told more than he realized, because everyone froze into silence. Milt handed the telegram to Cris. Nobody moved while she read. She handed the form back to Caleb and turned to Milt.

He never saw her more calm and serene, her gray eyes large and soft. "You'll be wanting to start in the morning. We'll need to rise early."

Caleb looked up from the telegram. "Win, you and your missus come on over to the house and wash up for supper. These young'uns got things to talk about. No need to cook tonight, Cris. Everybody eats at my place." Without waiting for agreement, he stuffed the telegram into his pocket, stepped off the porch, and climbed aboard his wagon.

Win assisted his wife back up to her seat on the wagon and swung into the saddle. Both of them wore grave expressions, but neither asked ques-tions. Milt admired their stern code. These were simply not the kind of people to intrude on oth-ers' troubles unless invited. Caleb snapped the reins and turned the team toward his home a couple of hundred feet away.

Cris said, "Caleb took your telegram."

"I know. I don't need it. He thinks fast, but he reads slow. Thanks for what you said, Cris, but I can't leave you right now."

"Milt, your brother needs you. Just having you

27

there will be immensely helpful for him. There's nothing useful you can do around here."

"You're getting close to your time, so my place is here with you."

She patted his hand. "That's sweet of you. I really need you to pace up and down the yard and chew your lip while I deliver my baby."

"Cris, even in a tight family, some have to be more important than others. You're the most important one for me. Until I'm sure you're taken care of I can't go anywhere."

"But you are sure. You and Caleb have already set up two relay camps between here and Victoria with fast horses held ready night and day. The doctor can be here in four hours. I guess it's not just coincidence that two of the best Mexican midwives in the county just arrived to visit our *vaqueros*. What more can you do?"

"How did you find out about the relay camps?"

"Milt, you're so simple sometimes. Did you really think you could do anything on this ranch without the women knowing about it? We know everything. Caleb's housekeeper and I do our washing together. She even knows how often you change your underwear, and if she knows, all the women know."

He stared off into the distance without speaking for several minutes. He knew a pause like that could seem like an unbearably long time, but he had no doubt Cris would wait without bothering him. Milton Baynes basked in the rare good fortune of a man who knew his wife understood him perfectly. She took his rough banter and teasing for precisely what it was, his way of expressing his love. He also knew she had a head as hard as granite once she made up her mind. Having decided, she would give him unceasing, undiluted hell if he didn't do her bidding.

Finally he turned to her. "Fact is, if I didn't go to him, I'm not sure I could live with it. You know the special feeling I've got for Ward."

"Yes, I know. He's the little brother you've felt you should watch over ever since your mother died."

"It's more than that, honey. I guess I should have talked to you more about Ward. He's not balanced like everybody else."

"What does that mean?"

Milt paused for a moment, groping for words. He had no idea how to answer that simple question, a question he'd never really answered himself. In the end, he decided he had to tell her something, even if he told it badly. This was no time for dodging. Cris deserved the most honest reply he could give.

"Most men feel fear for themselves and their family both. But Ward's all one-sided. He never seems to be scared for himself. It's like a part of him got left out of him when he was born. But when somebody in the family gets threatened, Ward gets scared ten times as much as an ordinary man. Instead of getting jumpy and nervous like other men do when they're frightened, he goes quiet and . . ."

"Kills. Is that what you're trying to say, Milt?"

"Yeah, and that may not be the best way to get Stitch back. They want money. That may be best."

"How much do they want?"

"You saw the telegram. Didn't say." At her quick nod, he asked, "How much do we have in the bank?"

"A little over fifteen thousand dollars."

"I'll take ten of it, just in case he needs it."

She nodded. "That's best. Money is no help in something like this unless you have it ready to hand."

Milt looked up to find Win Mill nearing the porch. Win tipped back his hat and said, "Put shoes on your wife if she has any. It's time for supper."

Cris slid forward. Milt planted both feet to steady the swing and cupped both hands at her shoulders while she eased her feet to the floor. His hands still hung in the air as if to preserve her balance until she padded into the house and slammed the door. When he turned back to Win, he saw Win looking at his upraised hands and dropped them quickly.

"Watching that, a man who didn't know better might get the idea you were fond of her."

Milt swallowed his embarrassment and said bluntly, "A man ugly as I am appreciates what he has."

Win smiled and leaned against a porch post. "Convenient, the way this is working out. I'm all packed and ready, so I don't have to kill horses catching up to you. My wife will stay with Cris. Eva's childless as yet, being a new bride, but she's a knowing woman. She'll be useful. Caleb says you'll be carrying a bunch of money, so I can help you look after it on the road to California. He says we can use the relays to town and then hit the road to San Antonio where we can catch the Butterfield stage. Says that'll get us there quicker than any other way."

"Sounds like you and Caleb got everything figured out for me. What's this about carrying money?"

"Caleb showed us the telegram, Milt. He said you'd strip the bank account. Anybody could predict that."

"Knowing man, that Caleb."

Win nodded, poker-faced. "I reckon."

"You sure you want to take this on, partner? This won't be a pleasure trip."

Win ducked his head and stared at the ground for a moment. When he looked up, his gray eyes held steady on Milt's. "I figure this is a family matter. If I'm family, I'm obliged to go. If you tell me I'm not obliged, I'm not family to your way of thinking."

Milt came to his feet, towering over the slight Win Mill, and spoke quickly. The slightest hesitation now could cause terrible hurt to this proud man. "You're family. I'm almighty proud to say it."

# THREE

Luke Baynes brushed his hands together and gazed with satisfaction at his new bookcase. A thing of beauty, by heaven, even if he did build it himself. He passed a soft cloth lightly across the spotless glass front, a caress rather than a search for smears.

Now his meager law library could grow in safety, with books easy to find and protected from the dust constantly floating in from the busy street. It soothed a man for his eye to pass over something fine, designed by his own mind and crafted by his own hand.

He rubbed his hands together again and glanced down at them. He had taken to wearing dress gloves lately to conceal the heavy calluses and scarred knuckles. Those hands simply didn't fit his position as a federal judge in Wyoming Territory. He stared at them for a long moment and decided not to bother with the gloves anymore. Something about wearing gloves in the summer made him feel like a fop.

In his court, he reigned supreme. If anybody disliked seeing the hands of a pick-wielding man, a prizefighter, a working-class commoner elevated to the bench, they could leave his court and sit in the street. He decided to stop hiding his hands under the table as often as he could at meals. Maybe serving as a judge made a man arrogant after a while. Maybe he felt he'd grown too big and important to pay attention to petty attitudes anymore. In any case, hands that could make a bookcase as sturdy and pretty as that one deserved respect, especially from the man who owned them.

A light tap on the door made him turn, and his fingertips brushed the holstered Navy at his hip. He chuckled, enjoying his private little amusement. What a collection of ingrained odd habits he had become. The slightest unusual event, even a knock on the door, and big Luke Baynes fondled his handgun, still on guard against threats long past. He'd probably still be doing that when he reached seventy, if he was so lucky as to last that long. Still grinning, he had a reassuring thought. Any fool who could laugh at himself didn't need to worry too much about becoming arrogant.

"Come in, Mr. Boniface."

The court clerk opened the door and took one step into the room. "I hate to disturb you in your chambers, Judge Baynes, but a telegram just came. I thought you might want to see it without delay."

Luke stepped forward to receive the yellow envelope. "Thank you. You might as well go on home. It's getting late."

"Judge, I don't want to intrude, but the telegraph man delivered that himself. He said he didn't want to trust it to the delivery boy. He looked most concerned. May I stay a moment, just to see if you need anything? I'm afraid it might be bad news."

Luke nodded and smiled at the stiffly formal young man. "Of course you're welcome to stay." He tore the envelope and flipped open the folded message. Luke read slowly, in the way of lawyers, trained to pay careful heed to each word, to let no implication slip past undetected. His heavy hands slowly tightened into white-knuckled fists, ripping the crushed message into two parts. He stared blankly at the wall beside his clerk, hearing his own labored breathing in the small room.

Then his head snapped up and his gaze met the clerk's. Boniface took a quick step away and was brought up sharply when his back slammed into the door. "My God, sir, you look . . . What is it, Judge?"

Luke closed his eyes briefly and forced his expression to soften. He'd let his mask slip for one unguarded moment, and he'd shocked his scholarly clerk. The young man had never seen the old

Luke Baynes. He'd only known the new one, the gentle student of law.

Luke forced his voice into a flat, controlled tone. "I have a family emergency, Mr. Boniface. Please clear my calendar for the next month. Notify the Justice Department that I shall be absent from the bench for . . ." He hesitated for a second before he finished with, "For at least thirty days."

"Of course, sir. I'll do that at once."

Luke forced his hands to steady as he smoothed the crushed telegram, folded the pieces neatly, and slipped them into his pocket. "If anything else comes up, handle it with your usual discretion and good judgment. I'll be leaving town as soon as I can catch a train."

"Where . . . uh . . . might you be going, sir? I'd like to be able to reach you, just in case."

"I'm not sure, but I'll start out by going to California. I'll try to keep in touch if I can, Mr. Boniface, but I don't know where this affair may take me."

Luke swept his hat off his desk and walked out with only a quick wave of a hand to acknowledge a quiet "Good luck, sir," from Boniface.

The short walk to his house seemed to take forever. He strode rapidly, nodding and tipping his hat to friendly greetings from those who passed. Rattled by the wild impulse to break into a run, he stopped for a moment to try to force himself into control, but grim thoughts crowded each other in their rush to torture him.

A two-year-old couldn't take much abuse from hateful people and survive. Little ones must be pampered and protected until their delicate little bodies could take hard times. Speed might mean everything. Even now, poor little Stitch might be suffering.

Ward, a living paradox, the most dangerous member of the family, was also the most easily hurt, the most vulnerable. He must be suffering beyond human endurance. Kit too, of course, but the iron in her could bend and spring back. With all her gentle ways, her nature provided greater strength to bear this kind of threat.

Poor Ward. His love for Kit, kindled and bluntly declared almost the instant he first saw her, rebuked a cynical world. Luke felt himself a man blessed simply to have been present to see their courtship. No man could watch such a thing without feeling a glow of hope for mankind.

When he came in sight of home, Helen sat in her rocking chair on the front porch, her sewing across her lap. Nancy Sands occupied Luke's rocker beside Helen. Both women smiled and waved, but Nancy's expression changed quickly, and she came to her feet. Her own sewing dropped in disarray to the floor. One step brought her to the porch rail. "Luke, what is it?" Nancy, with the eye of an eagle, always picked up signals others seemed to miss. She must have noted some tension in Luke's manner in spite of his effort to appear normal.

He paused for a moment, his glance shifting from Helen to Nancy, Helen's brother's wife. Helen's brother, Cotton, had once stood beside Luke in the middle of a darkening, icy, windswept street, both of them battered and bleeding, to face implacable enemies. That day of gunfire, pain, and death seemed remote now, but the bond formed would last forever.

"Telegram came. Somebody burned Ward's house and barn. They took Stitch. They want ransom." Luke's blunt words caused both women to flinch and straighten as if struck. He sucked in a deep breath. "I've got to go. I might be able to do something to help."

Helen came to her feet. "I'll be packed in an hour." She must have seen a flicker in his eyes, because she asked, "You didn't plan to go without me, did you?"

"I haven't planned much of anything. I'm not up to it yet." Both women stood waiting for his decision. "I guess that's why I made tracks for home so fast, to get some help." He took another deep breath. "I'll get my saddle from the stable. You throw something in a bag for us as quick as you can."

Nancy leaned against the porch rail. Standing there, her eyes were level with his. "I'm going to tell Cotton." At his nod, she came off the porch and hit the ground running.

Helen bested her promise by half an hour. Luke brought in his saddle. By the time he lifted his Spencer down from the mantle and cleaned it, she had changed into a street dress and shoved two carpet bags out of the bedroom and into the hall. She looked up at him, smoothed her almost white-blonde hair with a quick hand, and pinned her hat in place. "When is the next train?"

"I don't remember. I figured to go down there and wait."

"Good. I'll carry one bag. You get the other and your saddle. It's a short walk."

When they stepped outside, Luke saw the smoke from the train. "It's already here, Helen. We're going to miss it." They broke into an awkward run.

Cotton stood in front of the train station with Nancy. The small, almost delicate lawyer presented a picture of impeccably groomed and tailored assurance. Luke no sooner slowed to a halt in front of the two of them when Nancy lifted a holstered Navy and swung the hanging gun belt around Luke's waist. Her quick, agile fingers jerked the belt to the proper tightness and buckled it into place as if she'd practiced strapping a gun on a man all her life.

Luke stood as if thunderstruck. Nancy said, "I want you to bring that back to me." He couldn't think of anything to say, so he simply nodded. It seemed only yesterday that he'd loaned her his second handgun. Only minutes after receiving it she'd shot an outlaw, clean and dead center, saving Luke's life. She certainly picked a special moment to return the weapon.

Cotton said, "I have the tickets ready. Get

aboard." He turned, kissed Nancy, and followed them up the metal steps into the train car. They had no time to look for seats before the train clattered and lurched forward.

Luke grabbed Cotton's arm. "Cotton, we're moving already. Quick, you've got to get off."

Cotton gently brushed Luke's hand from his arm and smoothed his sleeve with an expression of mild disapproval. "I'm not getting off." He made a slight gesture toward the luggage rack. "Got my bag packed and everything." With an exaggerated flourish, he seated Helen and dropped into a seat opposite her.

Luke slowly settled himself beside Helen, keeping his eyes fixed on Cotton. "I guess you've decided to come along. Seems like you should have asked if we wanted to put up with you."

Cotton sighed, maintaining his expression of mild disgust. "One should not ask for decisions from backwoods rubes. It's better to be firm with them and guide their uncertain path."

"Thanks for getting the tickets for us, Cotton. We'd have missed the train."

"No, I asked them to wait for you. It only took a few minutes."

"They don't wait for anybody. How'd you get them to do that?"

Cotton shrugged and shifted comfortably on the hard seat. "They were nice about it, Rube. I just told them we'd kill them if they didn't wait. Railroaders are reasonable, surprisingly intelligent men. They all agreed waiting was the right

39

thing to do. I'm sure those efficient fellows will make up the time down the line." He smoothed his coat gently over the twin double-barreled derringers the garment concealed and then lifted a hand to stifle a yawn.

They rode in silence for a few moments before Cotton fixed hard gray eyes on his sister. He leaned forward and spoke as if Luke were not present. "You have made a decision that might need to be reconsidered. If we get Stitch back unhurt, little sister, everything will probably be all right. If he's hurt or lost, you may see things that will disturb you terribly. A blood feud ranks among the worst, most vicious things that can afflict mankind. Are you sure you want to come along? I can remember your pain when you first saw Luke's violent side. It might be better if you didn't see what might happen, at least not see it from so close."

Helen returned her brother's stare. She said, without hesitation, "I stand beside my husband."

After another pause, Cotton's eyes wavered. He said, "I spoke in kindness, but I see I presumed too much. I beg your pardon."

"Fine, your apology is accepted if you'll stop speaking to me as if I were another stuffy lawyer. I'm your sister."

"Agreed." He shifted his gaze to the silent Luke. "How much do we know about the situation, Rube?"

Luke pulled the telegram from his pocket and handed it over.

A moment passed while Cotton examined the torn document. Helen reached forward and Cotton gave it up. "I have no money, Luke."

Luke shifted restlessly and admitted, "I don't either, not enough to make any difference. I don't think that's important. Pa will help if need be, and Joe Thackery, his partner, will give Pa everything he has."

"That close, are they?" Cotton's question came in a mildly surprised tone.

Luke smiled. "Yes, they're that close, but that doesn't matter. Stitch is Thackery's grandson too, you know. He's Kit's father."

Cotton said, "I have been reminded. In my defense, I only met the man briefly when your family came to my wedding, and I forgot the connection. I was not my usual self at the time. Small, stiff, stern, quiet, gray, right?"

Luke nodded. "That's Papa Joe Thackery, no leaves, all thorns."

# FOUR

Darnell Baynes started across his ornate mahogany desk at Joe Thackery. The silence between the two men meant nothing. Long lapses in conversation merely indicated to knowing associates how comfortably the two men worked together.

Thackery, narrow face reflecting his habitual humorless expression, spoke in his usual flat tone. "Five hundred double eagles, all shining new, mint condition, all dated 1870." He indicated the bag of coins on Darrell's desk with a flicker of his eyes. "That order required real effort to fill, but our bankers responded like gentlemen when I told them the purpose of our demand."

"Trouble?"

"No, I think the panic is subsiding. President Grant ruined several hundred gold speculators

42

last month, and the markets are still vibrating. Fortunes were lost. Plenty of nervous nellies got rattled and lost confidence in the whole currency system. Everybody's calling September 24, 1869 'Black Friday.' When Grant announced he was going to sell government gold, he ruined Fisk and Gould's scheme to corner the gold market. I would say the president also effectively destroyed the rumor he was in on the scheme. Your kidnappers' demand for gold could have caused us a major headache, but hoarding doesn't make sense now with the government pouring gold into the market, so the bankers cooperated."

Darnell answered with a single word. "Backup?"

"Not yet. They're closest with a collection of 1868's. They have almost four hundred and fifty in hand. They can reach five hundred, but they'd have to use circulated coins to make up the difference. I told them to keep trying for all new ones." After another pause, he continued. "They can clean and polish the circulated ones so that you can hardly tell the difference. In extremity, we can make that do. They showed me how they do that. I couldn't tell polished circulated ones from the newly minted. Point is, I don't think we need to worry about obtaining more coins."

Thackery stopped speaking, but Darnell knew the man hadn't finished. Dealing with a man like Thackery took a special kind of patience. The important thing to remember was that Thackery never spoke unless he had something substantial to say.

"Paying for more coins than needed will hurt us, Darnell. We've used up all our signature credit. We'll have to sell assets or mortgage heavily. The only lucky stroke in this whole tragedy is those bastards don't know how rich we are. They probably named the highest sum of money they could dream of. Let's hope they don't find out they can have it all if necessary."

The two grandfathers sat again in silence for several seconds. That kind of silence signified complete, unreserved agreement in this partnership. When nothing needed to be said, nothing would be.

Darnell gently tapped the desk a couple of times with a meaty fist. "We shouldn't need another batch of coins. I hate to think we might have to pay a ransom twice. Still, accidents happen, and we have to be ready for bad luck. Just carrying this much gold is dangerous. Something about gold makes thieves out of honest men." He shook his head, a spare, almost invisible gesture. "Doesn't look like much, does it? Just a small, heavy canvas bag."

Thackery sat perfectly still, not even appearing to breathe. "Take a look at one of those coins."

Darnell lifted an eyebrow in question and asked, "You want to test my character, Joe?" but Thackery didn't respond, so he opened the canvas bag and took out a couple of coins. He looked closely at one, then the other. Finally, he looked up and shrugged. "Double eagles."

Thackery took a coin from his pocket and spun it across the desk. "Compare."

Darnell rose, Thackery's coin in one hand and one from the bag in the other. A couple of steps brought him to the window. He took his time and examined both, first one side and then the other. "All right, Joe. I see no difference. What's the trick?"

"Every coin in the bag has been altered, just a tiny change. I didn't want anything crude, so I hired a jeweler to do it. Look at the eagle side."

Darnell looked again for a moment but saw no difference. Thackery leaned forward and said, "I wanted something a person probably wouldn't notice unless the change was pointed out to him. Then the difference should be very obvious. You prove my point that the change isn't too conspicuous. I think this is going to work. The eye of the eagle has been polished away."

Darnell said, "Well, I'll be damned. I see it now."

"The change will make it easy for us to describe what to look for. We'll call those coins Blind Eagles. That'll make it easy for people to remember. If Ward turns over that money to somebody, we'll be able to recognize those coins afterward, no doubt about it. Still, you need to examine them in a good light to see the change."

"Not all that good, Joe, not when you know exactly what to look for."

"Precisely. My jeweler says, unless the men

we're after are unusually sophisticated about coins, they shouldn't notice anything. Since we're using coins minted this year, they haven't been circulating very long. Even if they notice the difference, they still might not suspect anything. The mint makes changes from time to time. You know there are several types of double eagles in circulation. I don't think we're up against coin experts."

"You're a crafty, devious, underhanded old man, Thackery."

"Guilty."

"And you make a perfect partner in all kinds of weather. I think it'll work, Joe, but we'll have to ask Ward's permission."

"Of course we do." Thackery sat back and folded his hands. "I'd fear for my life if we didn't. You do any good with your little projects?"

"I did, indeed. Surprised myself in fact. I never thought owning a few hundred shares of railroad stock would turn into such an advantage for us, Joe. Railroaders are a clannish bunch, and I guess our owning stock puts us on an inside track with them. They're ready to put it out on their wire. Within a few hours after we give the signal, anybody trying to pass one of those coins to a railroader will run into trouble."

"Anything else?"

"I wired Mr. Butterfield personally. He wired back his personal assurance that, as soon as we ask, he'll send the word along to every reputable stage line in the west. Anybody trying to pass one of those coins will get a gun shoved in his face and a demand to explain how he came by it."

"Kind of him."

Darnell caught a hint of wonder in Joe's tone and allowed himself a meager smile. Kindness from any source always seemed to surprise Joe Thackery.

"More than naive sympathy, I think. The thought came to me that I'm asking favors of rich men. They have families too. The notion of somebody grabbing his children and demanding money chills every one of those fine gentlemen. Only the wealthy can afford to pay enough to make a crime like this worth anything. This is an outrage that puts the rich and powerful on our side. Think about it."

Thackery lifted a cigar from the box on Darnell's desk. Darnell watched him go through the ridiculous, fussy procedure of preparation common to all lovers of fine cigars. He knew his partner used the meaningless activity to do exactly what he'd been advised to do. He was thinking. Cigar finally lighted and drawing satisfactorily, he stared at the trail of rising smoke.

Finally, he spoke. "Glad to have help from the rich and powerful *or* the poor and weak. Everybody's welcome. But I'd rather depend on my son-in-law. Ward's got a special gift and the sand to go with it," Thackery said.

"My worry about Ward is that he might be too fast with that gun, Joe."

Thackery said, "You Baynes men all carry a soft streak except Ward, so you worry about him busting loose like some kind of maniac. Nonsense. Ward's more like me, so I think I understand him better than you do." He added, "I say that without meaning offense."

Darnell impatiently waved off the thought, and Thackery continued. "He ought to be my son rather than yours. Ward and I hate better than you and your other sons. Pure hate gives a man strength, keeps him from being distracted. No man, unless he's a dullard, trifles with a good hater."

He drew gently on the cigar, blew a plume of smoke toward the ceiling, examined the inch-long ash. "I surely wish I could conjure up a way to claim that boy without casting aspersions on his mother's honor. I'd give him the Thackery name in a second. However, that would cause my daughter considerable dismay, so I'll settle for him being just my son-in-law."

"She looks mighty calm, Joe. Kit's a strong young woman."

"She keeps herself busy holding Ward back. Took all she had to keep him from riding off in all directions with blood in his eye. He finally admitted he ought to wait for us to collect the money, just in case he couldn't get Stitch back any other way. If he'd found a trail to follow, nothing she said would have stopped him, but he rode around for two days and came up empty. Riding around was good for him though. He needed to feel like he was doing something. Gave him time to get collected. Nothing wild about his attitude now. Just calm, cool, intelligent hatred."

"Milt and Luke should be along any day now."

"You heard anything from them yet, Darnell?"

"Heard from Luke. No need to hear from Milt. They're coming. They'll probably sneak in."

"Sneak in?"

"My boys all had the same training, Joe. They don't know friend from enemy in these parts. They'll come drifting in, maybe use false names, and creep up to my house like thieves in the night. I'll bet you a box of those cigars."

This time Thackery's expression was an unmistakable sneer. "You don't catch me in a dumb trap like that. No bet."

"As Milt used to say, he likes to decide whether he wants to kiss or kill before he shows himself."

Thackery pulled his watch from a vest pocket and glanced at it. "Time to go talk to that fellow Rudi again. He'll be expecting us."

Darnell Baynes rose without comment, locked the bag of gold coins in the safe behind his desk, and walked out ahead of Thackery. The short trip to Darnell's home passed without further conversation. They found Rudi propped up in bed in a narrow upstairs room.

Without exchanging greetings beyond sparse nods, the two men took seats beside the bed. Darnell spoke gently. "You feel up to going through it again, Rudi?"

Rudi answered quickly. "I feel a lot better, Mr. Baynes. I been thinking and thinking, trying to come up with something new that might help."

Darnell said, "I hope you can. I just have a feeling it's there, but you don't know it's important. You said they knew Ward's name, that they were looking for him. So I don't think this was done by passing tramps."

Rudi flinched and sucked in a breath.

Thackery put out a hand and said, "Don't jerk like that, man. Did you hurt yourself?"

"I just remembered what one of them said, Mr. Baynes. He said, 'We'll show them not to shoot a tramp.' I couldn't make sense of it, but what you said reminded me of it."

"Not to shoot a tramp?" Darnell asked. "What could that mean?"

Rudi shook his head. "I must not have heard it right, but he said it in English, plain as day. I been doing like you asked me to do, trying to re-member every scrap of talk I heard that day. Maybe if I could figure out one extra word it would make a difference."

Darnell met his partner's wide-eyed gaze. Darnell spoke in a thin, tense voice. "Maybe we have something, at last. What I'm thinking is un-likely, but it might be important."

"Rudi says all four of them were tall, light-skinned, sunburned, bony men." At this, Rudi nodded in confirmation, and Darnell went on. "There was a family we knew back in Louisiana that looked like that. One of them rode with the bunch of men that came out to the house the night we left home, and he got himself killed for it."

"What reminded you of them?" asked Thackery.

"Their name was Trampe. They spelled it with an 'e' on the end, but it sounds the same. I never ran across anybody else with that name. They caught a lot of teasing about it. They were not my kind of men, so we didn't socialize. Backwoods, ignorant folks, heavy drinkers and brawlers. I don't remember them being particularly unfriendly, but they kept to themselves. They mostly raised hogs and made whiskey. Seems like they came originally from Tennessee. There was talk they left trouble behind, but I never paid that kind of talk any mind."

Thackery said, "Sounds unlikely, even if you shot one of their kinfolks. That was years ago, and they've had plenty of time to cool. If they're Tennessee mountain people, they might be the feuding kind, but it's a long way from Louisiana to California. Don't most feuding men settle down if their enemies move out of the country? Why would they come after Ward way out here? Seems like they'd go for Milt in Texas first."

"Accident. We traveled all over, so they probably couldn't find us after the war. Milt made a splash when he went to Texas, but they might not have heard of him. Hell, Joe, people still call Milt's ranch Cowan's Fort. Lots of the local people around there don't even know Cowan sold the place to us. Suppose they came out here to look for gold and stumbled over Ward? The big rush is long past, but we see new gold prospectors wandering into California every day."

Thackery shrugged. "Still seems unlikely to me. Damned near every family in the country lost somebody during the war."

"Maybe so, but I'm going to warn my boys. They probably wouldn't even think of the Trampes being a danger. If I'm wrong, then no harm done. If I'm right, the boys need to know."

Darnell sat without moving for a few moments, wondering if he was letting his imagination carry him away. He finally rose and smoothed his coat. "One more thing about the Trampes; ignorant as they certainly were, they always had meat on the table. Drunk or sober, every one of them was as good with a rifle as a man can get."

# FIVE

Darnell Baynes sat at the head of his dinner table. The evening meal had passed quietly but not morbidly, a testimony to the character of his guests. Everyone seated at his table knew his rule not to talk of serious matters or of business during meals. Thus the conversation, except for a few awkward pauses, had an oddly normal tone under the circumstances, family and friends catching up on each other's lives.

The cook had departed, protesting mildly about being dismissed before she could wash the dishes and leave the kitchen spotless. The doors had been locked. The heavy curtains had been drawn all evening. His gaze touched each of his guests in turn, Joe Thackery, Ward and his Kit, Luke and his Helen, and Helen's brother, Roland "Cotton" Sands.

"We shall now talk of the trouble that has

brought us together." Darnell intended to keep his manner and speech strictly formal, regarding that as a way to defuse emotion and inspire clear thinking. He could feel the sense of relief in the room at once. All of them wanted to get at the only thing they could think about. Honoring his rule had been difficult.

"I congratulate you, Luke, for coming into town so inconspicuously, and I thank you, Cotton, for leaving your own affairs to come to our aid. We must take action soon, and I think we all need to know as much as possible so we don't make any mistakes. I've hired Pinkerton detectives to watch for anyone spying on my home. They have seen nothing suspicious so far."

Darnell turned to Luke. "I'll point them out to you. We are all wary. I don't want you to break their bones if you notice them hanging around. Ward knows them already."

Luke said, "Good idea."

Darnell came to his feet. "I'm pleased to report that Ward's hired man, Rudi Valdez, seems to be recovering remarkably well so far. Joe and I found out something from Rudi this afternoon. He heard one the raiders at Ward's home speak of tramps. He had no idea that might be someone's name, so he almost didn't remember it. I think the raiders might be members of the Trampe family from back in Louisiana."

Luke, scarred hands resting in his lap, said, "I shot a Trampe almost on our doorstep, Pa. One of them rode with that bunch that came after us the day Mama passed away, remember?"

Helen grew pale, but she sat quietly and stared at the tablecloth in front of her. Darnell wondered if Luke had ever told his wife that the Baynes family had killed six men the evening before they left Louisiana, six men who came on the Baynes's property on a wave of whiskey and hatred, determined to force his sons at gunpoint into the Confederate Army and to burn their home.

Darnell paused. He had heard that the eastern-born Helen was easily shocked, but he could think of no way to spare her. Odd, he could remember one cold day in Wyoming when he'd seen her own brother, Cotton, use a handgun with the kind of stoic efficiency that could only come from long and serious practice.

"Yes, son, I remember one of them died that night. They may have held a grudge all these years. It may be a false lead, but watch out for them, just in case. They are all lanky, tall men, with very light skin. They don't tan much, so they always appear sunburned." At their nod, he went on.

"This afternoon, Joe and I obtained, after some worrisome delay, enough gold to pay the ransom. The coins are marked." He nodded at Joe Thackery.

Joe came to his feet, pulled several coins from his pocket, and passed them around in pairs. When two coins lay on the table in front of each person except him and Darnell, Joe said, "One coin you have is marked. The other remains as minted. Examine them and try to find the difference."

They leaned forward to pore over the coins, lifting and turning them in the brightly lighted room. Joe waited until everyone sat back and indicated defeat before he spoke again.

"If I asked you to look for a blind eagle, would you do better?"

After several quiet exclamations of "Yes, now I see it," and "Of course, look at that," Joe said dryly, "I'd like the coins back, please. That's two hundred of my dollars floating around the table." With a murmur of amusement, everyone passed the coins back to him. He pocketed the coins, and returned to his seat.

Darnell said, "Ward and Kit must give their permission for me to use this trick. Would you like to have time to think it over?"

Ward turned to Kit. When she shook her head, he said, "We don't need more time." He said to Joe Thackery, "If the trick goes wrong, nobody gets blamed. We all have to take chances and do our best." His gaze returned to Darnell. "That's settled, Pa."

Kit said, "Thank you, Papa." Thackery nodded a wordless acknowledgment, his hard expression softening as it did every time he looked at his daughter.

Darnell continued, "We can obtain more coins, just in case these are lost, in case the ransom demand increases, or some other unexpected problem arises. I mentioned that I have

56

engaged the Pinkerton Detective Agency. I have given them pictures of all of us taken at Cotton's wedding last summer. I have pictures of the agents who will be working for us in and around Vallecito Stage Station." He passed a stack of four pictures to Joe Thackery, who began passing them on, one by one.

"Ward, I got these pictures because I don't want you shooting an agent we've hired. When these men see you, they'll try to keep you under observation. Do you understand?"

Ward nodded without comment.

"Joe, will you tell everyone about the arrangements we've made with the railroads and the stage lines?" Thackery rose, explained those details in his flat voice, and sat back down.

"Ward and Kit agree that the safest approach is to pay the money and get Stitch back, if we can. After we have him safe, we'll try to capture the kidnappers to make sure we don't have to worry about ourselves in the future. Our last priority will be to get the gold back."

Ward corrected his father. "Except I'm not interested in capturing anybody. I didn't agree to that."

Luke, the quick lawyer diverting a potential clash during sensitive negotiations, changed the subject. "Ward, do you have any pictures of Stitch?"

Ward shook his head. Kit said, "We've been working so hard. We just didn't think to take time."

Helen leaned forward to pat Kit's hand. "Of course. We'll tend to that later."

"I heard from Milt. He isn't coming." Darnell noted the shocked expressions around the table and corrected himself quickly. "I mean he isn't coming here. He and his wife's brother, Winston Mill, are heading straight to Vallecito Station. Milt couldn't get any gold, but he's carrying ten thousand dollars in paper money. He had no way to know how much we needed, so I suppose he's bringing what he could get quickly."

Helen asked, "Isn't that terribly dangerous for him, carrying that much money through all that wild country?"

Luke answered his wife with a smile. "Anybody who can take anything from Milt deserves all he can get. He'll have earned it hard."

Ward spoke again in the soft, barely audible tone he'd used all evening. "Milt's always trying to give me everything he has. Remember when he tried to give me his share of what we got out of the mine in Montana, Pa? Milt said the money would be a burden to him, he feared it would bring him bad luck, and he'd be obliged if I'd take it. He wanted us to have a good start."

Kit made no reply, but tears trickled from her eyes. She pulled a handkerchief from somewhere, wiped her eyes, and sat straighter in her chair. Darnell felt a swelling sense of pride in his youngest son's wife. Her loss of composure lasted only a few seconds. She bore her pain with silent dignity.

"This is what I think we should do," Darnell said. "Joe will stay behind. He'll accept and relay any messages. I'll ride out before light in the morning, heading for Vallecito. Ward rides out early, but in full light in case somebody's watching him. The word is that he's to come to Vallecito alone. Luke rides with Cotton, following a couple of hours behind Ward. Ward carries the gold. Anybody have any complaint with that?"

Cotton started to protest, but was interrupted.

Ward, still speaking in the soft, indifferent tone he'd assumed, said, "Cotton, all of us know the Trampes when we see them, and they know us. If you're riding with Luke, he can warn you if they show up. Riding two hours apart, we'll hear the shots if any of us runs into trouble. But if anybody wants me, I'll look like I'm alone. We stay close, but apart, even in Vallecito, if I get that far. Make sense?"

Cotton asked, "If you get that far?"

Ward replied, "We've got to figure they don't want to meet me at the stage station at all, that they plan to ambush me on the trail."

Luke asked, "Has anybody thought to go to the law?"

"Good question." Darnell hesitated. "With two lawyers at the table, I don't want to offend, but we don't expect much from the law. Maybe we just got out of the habit since we've spent so much time in wild country."

After a brief silence in which nobody moved,

he added, "I wired the governor of California asking assistance. He agreed to send descriptions of Maria and Stitch around the state. We really don't have much of a description of the kidnappers to offer peace officers." Darnell stared down at the table, knowing his answer sounded lame but having no idea what to do about it.

Luke dug into his coat pocket. He dumped six shiny metal objects on the table in front of him. "I brought a handful of United States deputy marshal badges. I'm ready to swear all of you in as deputies."

Shocked, Darnell sat down. "Can you do that, Luke, being away from your jurisdiction and all that?"

Luke answered, "I grabbed those on impulse when I left my office. Frankly, after thinking about it all the way here on the train, I'm not sure. I'm troubled about the propriety of it more than the legality." He glanced at Cotton.

Cotton's eyebrows rose as he caught the implied question. "You want a shoot-from-the-hip opinion?"

At Luke's nod, he said, "I can't think of a precedent, but I can't think of a specific prohibition either. I assume Luke's position is that this might not be good form, but the time to worry about that is later, after the fact. Seems like clear thinking to me."

"You think Luke might get himself in trouble?" Darnell asked.

Cotton smiled. "Mr. Baynes, lawyers don't like

to criticize each other except behind closed doors. Judges recoil in horror at the idea of criticizing another judge. Besides, they'll all sympathize with Luke's situation. Judges don't like people to think they have feelings, but they do. It's embarrassing, but it's a fact. Luke might get a mild reprimand someday, maybe twenty-five years from now, when the Justice Department gets through with studying and debating. Stitch will probably have a family by then, and Luke may already be on the Supreme Court."

Darnell asked, "If you were in Luke's place, would you do it?"

Cotton nodded. "Yes sir, if I was quick-witted enough to think of it."

Ward spoke, and everyone leaned forward to hear his soft voice. "I thank you, Luke. I'm in debt to everyone here for coming to help in my time of trouble. But I won't wear one of those. I'd as soon wear manacles and a ball and chain. The only law I'm interested in upholding right now is my own. I'll take no oath that might slow me down in doing it."

One of Luke's big hands curled around the badges, pulled them to the edge of the table, and swept them into the other. He dropped them into his pocket and glanced around the table. "I guess Ward speaks for us all?" When no one answered, he relaxed in his chair and smiled at Ward. "It was just a suggestion. I didn't have my heart set on it."

# SIX

SACRAMENTO, CALIFORNIA
NOVEMBER 4, 1870

Ward stood for a moment with his hand on Peepeye's saddle, his face turned away from the light of the lantern Kit held. His hands moved with reluctant slowness to pull the cinch tight. When he turned, he knew he had no choice about what he had to do next. He felt exactly as if he needed a running start to make a terrifying leap. Everything stood ready. His packhorse waited impatiently, pack secured. When he turned, all that remained to do was to face Kit and say good-bye. And he couldn't quite make himself do that yet.

Sunrise had passed an hour ago, but Kit's lantern came as a big help on a dark morning in a murky stable. Pa had departed two hours past. The time to make his move had come, but he tarried.

When he married Kit in a Montana saloon, his

bullet-torn cheek newly stitched and still afire from antiseptic, he'd sworn to himself that he'd never leave her side. He had fully intended to sleep beside her every night until he died in her arms, a contented man who had lived a full life.

Ward Baynes had also figured he'd never pull Jesse to shoot at another man again, not that having to do it bothered him particularly. Yet, something in him must have known better. He never broke the habit of practicing nearly every day but Sunday. He blinked when he realized for the first time, standing in his Pa's stable on a cold, clouded day, the ugly truth.

He realized he had never, ever thought of rolling Jesse's belt around his holster and putting him away. Jesse belonged on his hip, not in a closet or chest. Something deep and wise inside him had known Jesse would be needed again, but that something had been kind. It had kept quiet and let him have peace for a time.

"You're very thoughtful this morning. I feel you're already far away." Kit's tone came soft, intimate, like her quiet voice when they talked in bed after the lamps had been snuffed.

"I'm waiting for strength. Kit. I'm standing here staring at my saddle because I'm not up to turning around. When I turn, I have to say goodbye to you. I'm just not up to it yet."

"You will be. Don't push yourself. You always find courage somewhere. That's why I've always admired you. And that's why I've never feared you."

Ward's head snapped up, but he didn't turn. "Feared? Feared me?"

"Everybody fears what they don't understand, Ward. I never have understood how you can flutter and go near hysterical if one of your mares has trouble foaling. If you lose a foal, you vomit and grieve and can't sleep for days. You act like a scared, high-strung girl."

Her quiet tone was his property, his alone. He knew with absolute certainty that no other man had ever heard that special, loving toll of her heart's bell. The words didn't even need to have meaning. The tone was everything. He drank her voice like cool water.

He said sternly, "I don't flutter. I never fluttered in my life."

"You flutter, and your eyes get wet, and you fidget."

"I never."

"Then, when you get ready to face men who want to kill you, nothing happens. You go serene and quiet. How am I supposed to understand that, Ward? It's frightening."

Ward turned to face her. "It's confusion, and you know it. Like now. You could tell I was buckling under, and you talked crazy and got me confused. You know I can fight dragons bravely if I'm muddled enough."

She said, "Just don't get confused about what's most important. I want both of you back safe. If you can't bring Stitch back, my heart will break, but I'll live. If you don't come back, I'll die. Keep yourself safe, Kid Baynes."

Ward pulled on his gloves. "Good-bye, Mrs. Kid Baynes."

She stretched up and kissed him. "I love you, cold gunfighter with a soft heart."

"I love you too, crazy woman afraid of the man who loves you."

He stepped into the saddle, and Peepeye turned toward the wide stable door. The restless packhorse moved forward too quickly, came up and nudged the back of his leg. Ward reached down and shoved the eager muzzle back away from Kit. She walked beside Peepeye, her hand gripping Ward's boot until they came out of the stable shadows into the daylight.

Luke and Cotton stood, propped against the corral fence, mist from the damp morning darkening their hats and shoulders. Ward knew they had stayed away from the stable to give Kit and him a private good-bye. Luke stepped forward and raised his hand. Ward, because of his brother's great height, whipped off his right glove and gripped Luke's hand without having to lean from the saddle. Giant, quiet Luke said nothing. Ward didn't expect words from him. His eyes said it all. Then Ward leaned down to grip the hand of the small, dapper Cotton who looked frail next to the mighty Luke. Cotton followed Luke's example, said nothing.

Thackery appeared, like a grim shadow, dressed all in black. He made no offer to shake hands. When Ward pulled rein beside him,

Thackery looked up and said, "I'll give you the same advice I gave your father. Bury them to cleanse the land, but don't anger the Almighty. Say no prayer for them. The Lord despises a hypocrite."

Ward looked into the stern old man's burning eyes and said gently, "I'll save my prayers for you, sir. As long as you live I know my Kit will be safe."

Thackery's surprised blink equaled a lesser man's stagger of shock. He stiffened and walked to his daughter's side. Kit slipped her hand around her father's arm, but the stern old man kept his gaze on Ward.

Ward rode confidently, relaxed in the saddle, unable to bear even one glance back. With every stretch of Peepeye's magnificent stride, weight fell from his shoulders. He felt a ghastly grin wrinkle his rigid cheeks and breathed deep, savoring the fragrance of wet, rich earth. As he rode, eyes and ears alert and sensing everything with sparkling clarity, Ward's mind wandered. He considered his situation with cool satisfaction.

No rules of civilized behavior bound him now. All restraints fell away. No freedom compares to that felt by a man who sheds all motives but one. Abruptly, life attains an elegant simplicity, doubts vanish, confusion ends, fears fall away.

His son must be returned. Only the quest now mattered. If men helped, they would be rewarded. He would let them live. If men got in his way or refused help he needed, they would be punished. He would leave their unburied bodies behind. The quest could not be delayed for burials, little decencies, trivial tasks for those with leisure, for those who saw life as complex with many purposes and many responsibilities.

After four hours of mile-eating pace, Ward slid from the saddle and walked for an hour. Pa's tracks looked too fresh; no bent blades of grass had begun to straighten yet. Always a thinking man, he rode off the beaten path frequently, leaving a trail easy for Ward to read. Pa rode well, and he was superbly mounted. Still, Pa had a sturdy build, unlike Ward's lean frame.

Peepeye, with his unmatched strength and a light rider, would ride down any horse in the country, but his energy represented an asset to be hoarded. Given an even break, the stallion would catch any rider. Escape from Ward became impossible if he kept Peepeye fresh. Ward's awful grin widened. Pursuit would become recreation as long as he rode Peepeye, a ride unspoiled by tension, the end without doubt.

At noon, Ward stopped and let his horses graze by the roadside for an hour while he chewed a couple of hard biscuits with thick bacon folded inside. He sat with his back to a tree, wrapped in his slicker, and watched a slow rain, idly letting his mind wander. He felt his set, rigid grin soften when he remembered watching his wife pack a dozen biscuits for Pa in the early morning. She'd packed three for her husband. Two with bacon and one without, the plain biscuit for him to feed to Peepeye. Pa and Luke were the eaters in the family. Ward and Milt ate little, and both missed meals without distress.

The Baynes family surely must seem strange to outsiders. Pa and Luke, powerfully built, heavily muscled men, who could load more ore or cut more wood then most anybody, ended up doing soft work. Pa, a businessman, and Luke, a lawyer, earned their bread with brains. Ward and Milton chose to earn their living in the horse and cattle business, hard physical work. At least, Milton was tall as well as lean. Milt, actually, was twice as strong as he looked. Ward, with his small stature and slight build, should have chosen less challenging work, but no, he had to choose taming and training animals weighing half a ton.

Ward came to his feet, and Peepeye's head came up abruptly. Ward lifted the biscuit, and the bay came trotting to him at once. He got the whole biscuit. If Ward had tried to divide it with the gray packhorse, trouble would have erupted. Peepeye owned Ward, and he showed hostility if another horse received more than perfunctory attention. Little extras, like biscuits or sugar bits, came to Peepeye, now a member of the family, not to ordinary damn horses.

The ground rose gently as Ward rode east, but the rolling country offered no obstacle, and the trail soon turned south. The Sierra Nevadas now lay off to the left, but Ward felt no concern. The early cool weather hadn't turned to winter yet, but when it did, he felt prepared. He'd ridden through snow before, through cold country that would make a northern California winter look like mild summer. Besides, this country no longer lay as empty as before. Mining camps and ranches dotted the way, widely spaced, but available if he needed shelter.

Ward rode until nearly dark before he found a place to spend the night. He never considered anything other than a lonely campsite. His sparse fire to heat coffee died quickly, and he didn't bother to try to find or construct a camp shelter. His tarp kept the damp from reaching him from the soggy ground, and his slicker kept his blankets dry from the rain. He didn't even feel the need to unroll his old buffalo robe.

He lay awake long into the night, remembering the time when his whole family had gone months at a stretch, regardless of the season, without sleeping under a roof. Pa got so angry when they came up with body lice or fleas, as often happened when they took rooms in a town. Several times he'd talked about turning back to burn the infested places.

If Pa hadn't had such a feeling that turning back could be bad luck, the Baynes clan might have burned buildings from Mexico to Montana. Instead, they spent hours boiling their clothing and submerging other items in convenient streams for several hours to drown varmints. Ward remembered many an icy bath with strong soap that he'd just as soon have done without until the weather softened.

On this particular trip, Ward noted, Pa was riding cross country, avoiding the traveled ways. Without having discussed it with him, Ward decided he knew another reason besides plain habit. Ward often attracted attention for the simple reason that Peepeye drew admiration everywhere he went. Even the gray packhorse following Ward showed outstanding conformation and breeding.

Pa's house in Sacramento lay about a day's ride to the west of Ward's land. Pa, again without consulting Ward, had selected a route that swung wide and away from Ward's home. If his place had someone hanging around watching for him, they'd waste their time. Pa knew Ward had no desire to pass that scene of pain and destruction now. Besides, Pa had said many times that the best place to ambush a man was on his own doorstep. The most cautious men tended to relax when they neared home. The kidnappers would expect them to head directly south. Pa rode straight east for several miles, as if heading for Ward's place, before he abruptly turned south.

Ward knew better than to question his father's devious traits on the trail. It seemed perfectly natural, if they were to travel south, for his father to ride several miles in another direction first, especially when leaving a town.

He remembered Pa staring in pretended amazement at his youngest son. "Are you my son, or are you a stranger who looks like my son?" Pa had gentle and indirect ways of accus-

ing him of needing explanation when simple observation and experience should provide him all
the answers he needed. Pa encouraged his sons
to do their own thinking.

If someone wanted to have warning they were
coming, Pa didn't want to make it easy for them.
The dismal weather helped. Nobody rode in the
rain if offered a choice. Ward drifted to sleep in
comfort, thinking that his Pa had made both
warning and ambush nearly impossible. If somebody planned to take a crack at a Baynes, they'd
have to earn it the hard way.

# SEVEN

SACRAMENTO, CALIFORNIA
NOVEMBER 4, 1870

Helen said to Luke, "I don't think I'll ever be a western woman. I'm amazed at Kit. She watched Ward ride away as calmly as if this were an ordinary day in her life. How can she be so tough?"

"She's as tough as the need dictates," Luke said. "I guess all of us try not to disappoint those who depend on us." He slapped his saddle on a big black and bent to tighten the cinch.

"I'm not as rugged at Kit, Luke."

He looked down at her with a smile. "You don't need to be as much of anything as Kit. All you need to do is be yourself."

"I don't want you to go, Luke. I'm frightened to death."

"It's all right, Helen."

"You don't care what I think?"

"I care more than you want to know." He turned to her. "I'm going, and you know it. That doesn't mean you have to like it, nor does it mean you have to pretend to like it. It also doesn't mean I don't care what you think. It just means I have to do what I'm doing."

"Cotton warned me about you," she said.

"About me?"

"Yes. Before we married, he told me, sooner or later, I'd probably regret marrying a man of conscience. He said your kind of man doesn't listen to reason at times."

"Cotton means well. That was his nice way to tell you that you were about to marry a stubborn man. Fact is you've done mighty fine with it, seems to me, if having a happy husband is any measure. I'll bet Kit didn't act tough when she and Ward had their private good-bye. I'll bet that little snow maiden even shed a tear or two."

She stepped back with the smile that always seemed to make Luke's heart miss a beat. "I married a judge, a man wearing the best clothing those New York tailors could produce. Just look at you now, wearing two revolvers and all that rough clothing." She glanced at the rifle booted to the saddle on the black horse. "You look like pictures of bandits I've seen."

"Kinda romantic looking, ain't I?"

"No, just disreputable," she said.

"Well, I don't want to look prosperous where I'm going."

"I know, Luke. Get on your horse and go. I'm trying not to fall to pieces."

He kissed her and swung into the saddle. He

rode out into the light rain where Cotton sat in the saddle, patiently waiting, a stubby cigar in his mouth. One packhorse stood behind Cotton's mount, reins tied to his saddle. Without a word he passed the reins to the second packhorse to Luke. Luke attached them to his saddle, and both men kicked their horses into a slow walk. Luke looked back and waved to Helen, now standing in the muddy street, her golden hair protected by an upraised umbrella.

Cotton spoke in a low tone. "I'm carrying another five hundred blind eagles. Mr. Thackery came by while you and Helen were saying good-bye. He said the bank got them ready quicker than he thought they would, and the jeweler he hired worked all night on them."

"Pray we won't need them, Cotton."

"Agreed. Mr. Thackery said they wouldn't do a damn bit of good in a bank if we needed them."

"Mr. Thackery? My, my, aren't we formal this morning?"

"Damn right we are, Rube. I'm strictly formal with that old man. I'd hate to make him mad."

"He's already mad."

Cotton nodded, and raindrops fell from his hat brim. He reached up and removed his cigar, inspected it closely to be sure it was still dry, and stuck it back in his mouth. "Yeah, I guess that's what I mean. He's cocked and ready to fire."

"Me too. You still sure you want to ride with me? I wouldn't blame you if you had second thoughts. This is likely to be a blood trail."

Cotton said, "Wouldn't miss it for anything. You know, it's been almost a whole year since I shot anybody for trying to kill you, Luke. I wouldn't want to get rusty."

"That's a cute little joke. They were trying to kill you too."

"Yeah, but they wanted you most. You're bigger. You'd make a better trophy, being from an outlaw family and standin' nine feet tall and all that."

"Nonsense. Everybody wants to shoot a New York lawyer, especially a fancy-dressed little smart mouth like you."

Cotton went through the cigar inspection procedure again. "Yeah, I guess you're right. You know, you really hurt my practice by spreading the word around that I was honest. I never have figured out why you'd do me that kind of harm. No telling how many clients still avoid me because of that poisonous rumor."

"Sorry. I'll never do that again."

Cotton rode for several minutes before he asked, "Luke, how the hell do you know where we're going?"

"There lies Ward's trail, plain as day. We just follow it. We're only about two hours behind, so we don't even need to worry about the rain washing out his sign. If the rain picks up, we'll speed up and get closer so we don't have trouble."

Cotton said, "You know I'm not a rube like you. I never even shot a rifle in my life except for fun at my gun club in New York. Don't let me get lost out here in the jungle."

75

Luke's horse shied when he said, "Jungle? This is some of the prettiest country in the world."

"Looks pretty wild to me. I haven't seen a street sign in a long time."

"Don't worry, I won't let you get lost." Luke rode in silence after that, but he knew Cotton had not been making idle conversation. The man was a master at burying serious meaning in light-hearted sarcasm and apparent jest.

Regarded as the best pistol shot in New York by colleagues at his former law firm, Cotton has just reminded Luke that he was a city man. Steady of nerve and deadly as an aroused scorpion in a stand-up duel with pistols, he made no claim to being a woodsman. The trail that Luke read like a book in a strong light lay like a foreign language on a shadowed page for Cotton, a string of meaningless or even unseen marks on the ground.

"Cotton."

"Yeah?"

"Relax and concentrate on watching everything around you. We'll be on the trail for days. I'll point things out for you. Ask questions, especially the ones you think sound dumb. The dumb questions usually are the most important. I'll show you hand signals my family uses all the time. Most of these things only need to be seen and explained once to be understood forever. Once you see the north star, you never have trouble finding it again, right?"

"Right."

The mere fact that Cotton answered without some kind of sarcastic rejoinder signaled that he was listening with complete seriousness of purpose.

"Learning wood lore can take years if you have to learn everything by experience. You'll be shocked how much and how fast you can learn with somebody pointing things out and explaining them. In just a couple of days you'll find yourself feeling more comfortable out here where there are few street signs."

Cotton examined his soggy cigar, tossed it aside, and said in a slow drawl, "Ain't it amazin' how a man's mind opens to larnin' new thangs if his life is at stake?"

"When we camp, forget your cigars. I can smell one a hundred yards away. My brother, Milt, can smell one from almost twice as far. We just better hope we don't come up against anybody like Milt."

"Do you think we might?"

"Not if they're white men."

"I wish he was with us."

"I don't think he's had time to get here from Texas yet, but with Milt you never know. Milt could be with us right now. He doesn't always see fit to show himself."

Cotton chuckled. "You make your brother sound like a strange fellow, Rube."

Luke looked straight at his friend. "Lesson number one, Cotton. Both of my brothers are strange. Don't forget that. Not for one minute."

# EIGHT

Near Vallecito Stage Station, California
November 16, 1870

Micajah Trampe pulled his horse to a stop and sat staring into space for several minutes. He pulled off his wide-brimmed hat and rubbed his head and face, knowing his dense gray hair and beard fluffed into a disordered cloud. The more he thought about what might be happening behind him, the more a flush of anger heated his gaunt features. His gaze dropped and he watched his own long-fingered hand whiten with his tormented grip on the pommel of his saddle.

He slapped his hat on and spoke to his oldest son, sitting with his usual patient and silent manner beside him. "Fane, stay here. I'll be back directly." He jerked the horse around and started down his own back trail.

With every step, his anger rose until his breath roared from him like a man running. Justice, all he wanted was justice, but bad luck tracked him like a blood curse. His many failures he could bear. The Lord gave no promises, and Micajah expected no favors from Him. But no righteous man should be troubled with sons so treacherous, weak, and stupid.

Only Fane justified Micajah's trust. Smart, cool, and dependable, Fane almost made putting up with the other two bearable. Jole had no more backbone to him than a blade of grass, sneaky and underhanded he was. That boy was worse than a rutting bull with the attitude of a savage pagan, but without the grace of courage. That left poor Arlo, so painfully stupid he could hardly be trusted to boil beans. Arlo killed his ailing mother on his way into the world, and he'd never get along without somebody looking after him. He looked normal enough, but he'd be simple all his days.

Micajah had hardly ridden out of sight of the abandoned cabin before this grim suspicion overtook him. Worst of all, he knew a moment's carelessness of his own caused his discomfort. The thought that he couldn't forget his own son's foul nature, not even for a moment, made him grind his teeth. He kicked his mount into a gallop.

In front of the cabin, Arlo sat with a pleased smile on his face, playing with the Baynes whelp. He looked up, his face alight with artless joy. "Paw, you come back already."

"I told you to stay with the woman and the child. Where's the woman?" Micajah walked past him toward the cabin before Arlo could respond.

Arlo, blinking, face gone tense, gathered Stitch in his arm. "Jole told me to go outside and play. He said I could play with the baby."

Micajah shoved open the door and stepped inside, pistol in hand. Jole lay on top of the woman in the middle of the room, tearing at her clothing, framed in a rectangle of light from the open door. He struggled to his feet, looking down, trying to button his pants, and never even looked up to see the pistol in its vicious, chopping arc. The wicked blow snapped his head to the side and drove Jole to his knees. Micajah saw a trail of flying blood drops sprinkle the woman's white petticoats from the first blow before he swung again. Jole dropped on his face.

Micajah crouched over the woman. "Did I get here in time?"

She sat up and pulled her dress together at her neck with one hand. The other hand drifted to her mouth. Her gaze lowered, and she looked at the stained hand she drew away from a bleeding lip.

"Did you hear me?"

She nodded.

"Answer me, woman."

She nodded again.

"Speak."

"Yes, in time."

"Are you hurt?"

She shook her head.

"Woman, when I ask a question, you answer me."

"No, not hurt." She straightened a leg, pushing herself farther away from him. Holding her dress together at the neck with one hand, she tugged her skirts down with the other.

Jole stirred and groaned, one hand groping at his bleeding head. Micajah swiftly straightened and in two steps stood over his son. His pistol rose and fell again. The grisly crack brought a muffled gasp from the woman. He raised his voice. "Arlo."

"Yeah, Paw?"

"Bring my rope. It's on my saddle, Arlo."

"I'll get it, Paw. I can do that." Arlo appeared in the door quickly, the baby cradled on one hip, the rope draped over his extended free hand. His wide eyes darted from his father to the prone Jole to the woman.

Micajah drew the skinning knife from his belt and cut a short length from the coil of rope. He jerked Jole's hands behind him and swiftly tied them, jerking the binding brutally tight. Another slash of the blade and another piece of rope came from the coil. He bound his son's feet together. He straightened, one hand at the small of his back, and stretched. He swung his head so quickly toward the woman that she flinched and shrank from him.

"Your name's Maria, ain't it?"

"Yes."

He grunted, an explosive, nasal sound, and

continued to stare at her for a moment. Finally, he said, "This here won't happen again."

She didn't look away like he expected. Instead, she met his stare until he had to look away. That embarrassed Micajah more than anything else that had happened. A man shouldn't ever have to let himself be stared down by a woman. It wasn't fitting. He could still feel the burn of her accusing gaze, and his anger toward Jole flared brighter. His rutting son acted like a beast, and that humiliated him so much he couldn't even meet this Mex woman's eye.

He grabbed the rope binding Jole's hands and lifted sharply. Jole's body rose from the dirt floor except for his dragging feet. The fierce backward pressure on his arms and shoulders brought a moan from the half-conscious Jole. Micajah dragged him outside to the base of a tree, his son's face and feet dragging in the dirt. Swiftly, he tied one end of his coil of rope to the binding between Jole's wrists. A quick flip of the rope over a branch, a couple of powerful pulls, and another tie completed the job. Jole now stood with his bound hands pulled far up behind his back, legs trembling even though his boot toes barely touched the ground. Micajah cut off another six feet of the rope.

"Arlo."

"Yeah, Paw."

"Go get me a bucket of water from the well."

"I can do that, Paw."

As soon as Arlo trotted to him with the bucket,

he walked inside the cabin. He put the bucket on the table without looking at the woman. "Wash your face. Do it now. I want that water soon's you're done with it." He jerked open Jole's saddlebag and pulled out his son's best shirt. Again, without looking at her, he extended the shirt in her direction. "Put this on."

She lifted the shirt from his hand, and he stood staring out the door until she said, "You can have the water."

He grabbed the bucket and stepped outside. He walked around in front of Jole. With his arms pulled up at a cruel angle behind him, the boy's face hung toward the ground. Micajah stood patiently waiting. As soon as Jole's head came up, Micajah grimly peered into his son's eyes. "You see this?" He raised the bucket.

Jole blinked for a second or two but didn't answer.

"You see this?" Micajah asked for the second time, his voice commanding and harsh.

"Yeah." Jole's answer came slow.

Micajah held up the six-foot length of rope he'd cut. "You see this?"

"Yeah." Another slow, vague response.

Micajah put the bucket on the ground and twisted the short rope into a tight loop. He jammed the loop into the bucket. "After a while, the notion will come to you that groaning and moaning will get you sympathy." He lifted the dripping rope from the water and held it in front of Jole's face. "This here's called a sympathy

83

rope. You want some of it right now, just to get the feel of it?"

When Jole shook his head, a barely noticeable movement, Micajah doubled the wet rope and swung it. The rope hummed on its way. The doubled end smacked solidly against Jole's cheek. Like a man awakened, Jole's sagging knees straightened and he whined. "Don't, Paw. Don't hit me no more."

"You forget yourself, boy. When I ask a question I expect you to answer me. You forgot how to be respectful?"

"No, Paw. I ain't forgot. Don't hit me no more."

Micajah twisted the rope into a tight loop again and dropped it back into the bucket. He turned to walk away, but a groan of pain escaped from Jole. Without hesitation, Micajah spun around, pulled the rope from the bucket, and said, "Time for sympathy. A moaning man needs sympathy." Jole's pleading cries stopped when the doubled rope cracked across his head, leaving a streak of blood streaming from one ear.

"Hang there thanking the Lord for your luck. I got here in time, so I might let you live. I ain't decided in my mind yet what to do with you. In the old days, I'd have to stone you to death. That's the way the righteous treated rapists, fornicators, adulterers. You think on it." Micajah turned away.

"Arlo."

"Paw?"

"Don't go near Jole, you hear me? Jole's got to

hang there. No matter how much he begs, you don't go near him."

"No, Paw, I won't go near Jole."

"You make the woman stay in the cabin. You watch the baby. They better be here when I get back. Now, what did I tell you?"

"I don't go near Jole, no matter how much he begs. I make the woman stay inside. I watch the baby."

"I'll be back before nightfall, Arlo. I'm depending on you."

"I can do that, Paw. Can I play with the baby?"

Micajah mounted and sat staring at Arlo. Finally, he nodded. The lad could handle it. About three instructions were his limit. Otherwise, he got confused. Micajah lifted the reins and turned his mount. He still had work to do.

Fane sat on his heels, not ten yards from where Micajah had left him, smoke from his cigar rolling up and over his hat brim. As Micajah drew near, Fane came to his feet and swung into his saddle.

"Your brother went for that Mex woman. I should've known better than to leave him around her with only Arlo to keep him under control. Why didn't you say something? I got to do all the thinking, can't get no help from the likes of you?"

Fane, cool and distant, spoke around the cigar in his mouth. "You didn't ask, Paw."

"Don't get smart with me, boy."

Fane rode with his eyes straight ahead.

"You hear me, boy?"

Fane reined in and turned to face his father. "You whipped me twice in my life for offering suggestions. Whipped me so bad I suffered from it for a couple of weeks. I don't offer anymore unless you ask. I keep my mouth shut. That's the way you want it. You want it different now, say so right now."

"You telling me what to do nowadays, boy?"

Fane's eyes didn't waver. "I am."

Micajah actually reeled back in the saddle. He couldn't have been more shocked if his son had struck him. "What? What did you say?"

"I said I'm telling you what to do. You stop calling me boy. You listen when I think I got something to say. It's that or I ride my own way, starting now. You decide."

"I think I need to take a rope to you too. I just got through taking one to your brother."

"Paw, you can try. I owe it to you to tell you, man to man, how it'll be. You take a rope to me again, I'll kill you or die trying. You decide. You got a man for a son, not a boy. The boy part's finished. Finished right now."

Micajah swallowed. His throat, in an instant, had gone stiff and dry. Fane's blue eyes never wavered, and they had gone flat and shiny as glass buttons. Micajah found his own gaze shifting, and a cold chill struck him when he noticed the tie-down thong for Fane's pistol hung loose beside the holster. His son's hand dangled, relaxed, beside the pistol.

"You ready to draw on your own paw? Is that what I'm seeing?"

"You're the head of this family. You decide what happens here today, Paw. I ride with you as a man, or I ride alone from here on. I done my thinking on it. Now, you do yours."

"I can't believe my own son's sitting there ready to draw a gun on me."

"Decide, Paw. You're gabbling like a broody hen."

Blood rushed to Micajah's head so hard he felt his face grow taut, and pressure behind his eyes brought on a dull pain. "Insults. You think you can insult me and get away with it."

"I do. And I'm done talking." Fane reined his horse around and started down the trail.

"Wait."

Fane's horse kept walking.

"I decided, Fane."

The horse stopped.

"I could use a good man in my family."

The horse turned. Fane sat, waiting.

"I don't think you're done talking, Fane. Speak your piece."

The horse ambled back until Fane brought it to a stop with its nose at arm's length from Micajah's.

"I don't think us burning a man's house and barn is righteous. Shooting an unarmed man we never even saw before is a coward's doings. Taking a woman and child and running off with them is work for savage heathens. I've rode this far with you because blood kin is blood kin. That's finished. I'm shamed by all this."

"Shamed? You telling me you're ashamed of your own paw?"

For a long time Fane stared, long enough that Micajah felt beads of sweat slide down his ribs.

"All my life I've listened to you say that a man shouldn't have to say things twice. Poor simple Arlo could understand what I said. I ain't going to say it again."

Micajah dismounted and pulled a bottle from his saddlebag. "Looks like I got me a straight-talking new man in my family." He lifted the bottle toward Fane, but he shook his head. Micajah took a drink while Fane stepped down, and they both sank to their heels.

"Paw, there's a lot I never told you about Burl. You never would let me say anything. Every time I'd try to tell you anything you'd jump up howling like you'd set yourself down on a hot branding iron. It's time you heard the real story."

"You about to speak ill of your dead brother?"
"I am."

Micajah nodded slowly. "All right, son. We got us a new deal, you and me. Spit it up. You sound like it's been souring in your gut for a long time."

"Paw, Milton Baynes beat Burl one night at a dance. He whipped him like he was nothing. He whipped him without even marking him, kept thumping him in the belly till Burl couldn't even stand up. Burl never landed a blow, not one. Most pitiful, one-sided fight you ever saw. I started to step in to help him, but that big Luke Baynes smiled at me and shook his head. I swear, Paw, it was a friendly smile, like a man wears when he says, 'Glad to oblige.'

"I saw Luke hit a man one time, and they couldn't wake that feller up for three or four hours. I heard it was a week before that feller got over dizzy spells good enough so he could work. I didn't want any part of Luke, Paw. I just didn't have it in me to take him on."

Micajah took another small sip from the bottle. "So Burl got a whipping. Nothing there to cause fever. Happens to everybody, mighty near, from time to time. Young bulls like to butt heads."

"Burl was as bad as Jole, Paw. Didn't have the sense of a wild jackass around girls. He grabbed at a girl Milt was dancing with, and Milt took him outside and thumped him like a drum. I saw Burl put his hands on that girl, and I was so ashamed I would have whipped him myself if Milt hadn't done it. He brought it on himself, Paw, but he hated Milt like poison." Fane gestured toward the bottle, and Micajah handed it over.

Fane let the bottle hang from a relaxed hand and looked his father straight in the eye while he spoke. "Burl was more'n half drunk when he rode to the Baynes house that night they killed him. He didn't go out there with that gang of fools to get those Baynes boys to join the army and go fight the Yankees. He went out there figuring to kill Milt."

"You knew about it?"

"I did. Burl wanted me to go with them. I told him to go to hell, and I came home. Burl asked for what he got, Paw. I been wanting to tell you this for years."

"Don't make no difference, son. A blood debt is still a blood debt."

Fane's eyes finally dropped to the ground in front of him, and Micajah had to resist the urge to sigh in relief. His son's steady gaze today tended to give him a chill and make him sweat at the same time.

"All right, Paw. I'll tell you straight. I got nothing against them Baynes men, but I don't mind killing them if you'll feel better about it. But this other fooling around ain't decent. We shot a stranger, just because he was standing there."

Micajah snorted and spat. "You upset about shooting a damn Mex?"

"He was a man, Paw."

Micajah met his son's eyes for a moment. Then he flipped a hand to dismiss the subject.

Fane continued. "Then we took that little Mex woman. She don't have nothing to do with us. And that baby boy, now ain't that a proud thing? We putting a blood debt on the head of a two-year-old baby, Paw?"

Micajah joined his son in staring at the ground in front of him. "Didn't figure to harm the baby or the woman. I figured to kill that Ward Baynes and ride away. That would end it. One of us. One of them. Even."

"Then how come we done all this other?"

"I had it come to me when that baby's daddy wasn't home. It just came to me that we could get him to come to us, and we could maybe get us a bag of gold at the same time. Them Baynes men has always had devilish good luck with money, damn them."

"Why shoot that Mex? He was just there sparking that woman. That was plain as the nose on my horse."

Micajah took a tired breath. "I can see shooting that damn Mex sticks in your craw, but I can't figure why. If it's so big a thing to you, I'll tell you. I shot him because he had a bad eye, son. He wasn't wearing a gun, but you can bet a day's work he had a knife. All Mex's carry knives, and that one had a proud look in his eyes. He was one of them fighting kind of Mex's, could tell by looking at him, so I figured we'd have to shoot him anyway. So I done it and got it over with. At least, by doing it quick before he hopped onto one of us with a blade, I didn't have to kill him."

"All right, Paw. What's done is done. I still don't see no reason for a blood debt. Burl took it to them. I can't see no blood debt when them Baynes people was just defending themselves. Don't make sense to me, Burl being a damn fool like he was. He forced them to it. No getting around that."

Micajah sat in silence with his thoughts while Fane finally lifted the bottle and took his usual meager taste. He smacked the bottom of the bottle on the ground a couple of times to make sure it would stand straight before releasing it.

Fane struck a match, put the flame to his cigar, and slacked into patient waiting for his father's decision.

"You think we ought to take the money and not do any killing?"

"You want to kill somebody, Paw, I don't mind. It ain't that. I just don't think it needs to be called a blood debt. Seems to me a blood debt is a responsibility that can't be dodged. Puts a burden on a man that might get to weigh heavy. A simple killing, now, that's just a thing can be done if it's necessary. It ain't like it's no obligation or nothing like that. I'm more inclined to get the money, if we can, and ride on without killing nobody unless it's needful."

"You think we can take money from a Baynes without killing him, son?"

"Paw, if it's needful, I don't see no reason to grieve about it. We agree, do we? The money is the thing to go for? The killing ain't important?"

"I've got to give that some more thinking, son. I ain't got all you told me chewed enough to swallow it yet."

"All right, Paw. Let's just say I want the money, and you want the killing."

"Wait a minute. I ain't saying I don't want the money."

Fane smiled for the first time. "Paw, I think when you ponder on it, you'll come to the same notion as I have. All this other wind and thunder means nothing. The real lightning strikes where the money lies."

# NINE

The tracks overlaying Pa's troubled Ward. Two riders without pack animals crossed Pa's trail and abruptly changed direction to follow him. Pa's route took him over ground no other traveler would select except, perhaps, for a short distance. This country showed the clear signs of settlement, with roads and heavily traveled routes. Pa had elected to ride cross country.

Ward urged Peepeye into a canter and cast an appraising eye toward the afternoon sun. He figured he had time to catch up before dark with time to spare, given his father's leisurely pace. Knowing Pa's trail-wise habits kept him from being too worried. Those riders would have an unpleasant shock if they figured to overtake Pa and take him by surprise. The man who taught Ward the value of watching his back trail would hardly violate his own teaching.

The rain had stopped last night, with the morning dawn coming sweet and clear. The wet ground made trailing him from horseback easy. The countryside now opened up, with more clean grassland, low but rich forage usually standing only about a foot high, broken up with frequent clumps of trees. Every mile of southward travel took them into drier country. Ward slowed for a moment and leaned from the saddle. The tracks of the men following his father showed distinct indications of faster riding, deeper and with longer strides than Pa's.

Ward pressed Peepeye into a faster pace. He had no intention of letting his Pa face, all by himself, two men of unknown intentions. Even if he readied himself, Pa would have to defy bad odds if Ward couldn't come up in time. If the men he followed were up to no good, Ward figured they would try their tricks at dusk or even wait till nightfall. Creeping into a lone man's camp would give a bandit a chance to get close, to get the drop on an unsuspecting victim. Many a careless man had let himself get caught exposed in and blinded by the light of his own fire.

A quick inspection showed Jesse was ready for action. Ward dropped him back into his holster but didn't refasten the tie-down thong. The tracks looked fresh, a hot trail. He pulled Nadine from her boot, cranked a shell into her chamber, and rode with her cradled across his chest, thumb on the tang of her hammer. He could have her cocked and ready to fire during his swing onto a target. Only minutes behind, Ward expected to see his quarry any second.

The sight of them came just before he broke out of a wood line. The two rode close together, one leaning from the saddle with his attention focused on the ground. They were only a couple of hundred yards ahead, riding across an opening toward another wood line. Ward's breathing eased, and he felt a bit of wonder at his own sense of satisfaction. He had arrived in time, and neither of the men he trailed showed sense enough to spare a glance to their rear. Ward had been taught more caution when he was a boy in knee pants than these men displayed.

No doubt remained that his reading of the tracks had told him the correct story. These men were on his Pa's trail, and Ward could think of no innocent reason for that. Thus, there remained no question about what needed to be done.

Ward eased Peepeye to the left to follow the edge of the woods around the clearing. If those men should look back, he didn't want to get caught in the open with his quarry already hidden in the woods on the other side. Peepeye, agile as a deer, dodged and swerved through the trees without slowing, his hooves making little sound on the soft ground. Ward never rode with loose rigging that rattled and jangled, nor did he use fancy gear with shiny ornaments when he rode wild country. He didn't expect the men he followed, intent on Pa's trail, to detect him.

Ward judged the speed at which he'd last observed the men traveling and guided Peepeye to swerve around in a loop to get ahead of them. He came to the edge of the woods at the next spacious opening and drew rein. Pa's horses, saddle and pack removed, grazed peacefully in clear sight on the far side, only a hundred yards away. Ward felt a grim smile stretch his tense face. Pa stopped and put out decoys while good shooting light remained, exactly as Ward would have done.

Ward dismounted and dropped the reins. Peepeye stood still as a statue, head up and alert, breath coming quiet and easy, looking at Pa's horses. Long training held Peepeye silent and still when he saw Nadine in Ward's hands, and the dropped reins would hold him ground hitched for hours. Since Ward, when he was thirteen years old, had helped pull Peepeye from his dam, not a day had passed without the two of them spending time together. After a ten-year partnership, both man and horse knew what to expect from the other.

Ward moved forward, scanning the woods and stepping with all the care of a man trained to stalk since childhood. The lowering sun threw slanting rays of serene, yellow light across the land, and a soft evening breeze set the brush into gentle movement. Only a few minutes of cautious progress brought Ward a view of the men he wanted, and he felt another flicker of contempt.

They rode within a few yards of where he expected to find them. If these men had plans to act like highwaymen, they had little to brag about. This kind of predictability on the trail marked them as poor woodsmen. Ward stood motionless and watched while both men drew rein at the sight of Pa's horses grazing in the open. They pulled out their rifles, slid from their saddles, and crept to the edge of the brush.

They knelt side by side at the edge of the woods, less than fifty yards away, rifles drawn to their shoulders. The barrels of both rifles drifted back and forth as they searched for a target, so intent on their own hunt that they had no inkling they were also being hunted. The fools didn't even have enough sense to separate. They knelt almost shoulder to shoulder.

Long past hesitating, Ward drew a careful bead and shot one of the men through the head. The force of the bullet slammed him against his partner before he dropped to the ground. The other man, knocked off balance and splattered with blood and brains, froze in shock for a critical second, looking down at the smashed head of his partner.

Ward levered in another shell and shot him through the side, chest high. The man came to his feet, shoulders hunched, stumbled blindly for a couple of steps, dropped his rifle, and fell on his face. Ward cranked in another shell and lined his sights on the struggling man when he rose without his rifle and staggered a few more steps before he buckled to his hands and knees. Ward watched him for a few seconds, but the man didn't rise again. Instead, he slowly crumpled until he lay flat, facedown.

Ward called, "Pa?" He slipped two rounds into Nadine's magazine and gave her his habitual, affectionate pat on the butt.

"I'm here, son." His voice came from the woods beyond his horses. Pa's deep voice sounded calm and carried easily over the distance.

"Did you know they were trailing you?"

"Yeah, boy. I figured seeing the horses would bring them in close. I hoped to get the drop on them and find out why they were dogging me. Then I saw they had rifles already up and ready, so I was in a stew. I couldn't get a clear shot at both of them unless I moved, and I didn't want to do that for fear they'd see me and start shooting."

"I think they're both done, Pa. Let me check before you show yourself."

"We'll check together. Are you sure there were only two of them?"

"Yes, sir."

"Can you see both of them?"

"Yes, sir, I can. The first one got his through the head. No need to worry about him, I think. The other took a shot through the body. He's lying still, but he's the one worth watching."

"He's the one I can see, son, the one you got with your second shot. I'll watch him. You watch the other, all right?"

"Let's get at it, Pa." Ward stepped forward,

Nadine already at his shoulder and cocked, eyes on the downed man, knowing without chancing to look that his father was coming to join him.

Hardly a glance sufficed to verify the head-shot man would cause no trouble. The other groaned when Pa gently rolled him over on his back. He coughed and spat blood when Pa lifted his shoulders and supported him in a sitting position.

Ward knelt beside the man and said, "You're hit bad, man, shot through the lungs. There's no hope for you, and you don't have long. Who are you?"

When no answer came, Pa asked, "Do you have family you want told?"

The man shook his head. His voice came hoarse and weak. "Never mind my name." His chin dropped to his chest for a moment, and Ward thought he was gone, but his head lifted again and he spoke. "I got no family that gives a damn."

"Why were you after me?" Pa asked.

A spray of crimson from his nose speckled the front of the man's shirt as he struggled to breathe. A wracking cough shook him and he spat blood again before he answered. "Saw your partner pick up gold at the bank. Me and him," he nodded toward the dead man, "we figured you to be carrying it somewhere. We saw you leave town. We rode like hell to circle around you and set an ambush, but you turned off in a different direction. We rode a big loop till we cut your trail again."

"How did you see my partner pick up the gold?"

Again, the wounded man nodded at the dead one. His answer came in short gasps. "He worked at the bank. Got fired. Figured to get rich. Said you'd never . . . take that much gold . . . unless you were going . . . someplace with it. Worthless town man. I had to do it all. He couldn't trail . . . a gut-shot deer . . . across a snow bank."

Pa said, "You sure you don't want to tell us your name?"

When the man didn't answer, Ward reached down and lifted the man's head. The eyes were fixed. Ward glanced up at his father and shook his head. Pa lowered the man's shoulders to the ground.

Pa said, "I guess we have a burying to do."

"Why bother, Pa? We got more important business to tend to than burying cheap crooks. In fact, I already decided not to let this kind of thing trouble me until I get Stitch back."

Pa rubbed his face and took a deep breath. "I'll do it. I brought a shovel."

"What did you bring a shovel for?"

"I figured I'd need it sooner or later." Pa's gaze met Ward's. "Figured right, didn't I? You don't have to help, son, if you can't see your way clear to do it."

Ward met his father's eyes for a moment before

he said slowly, "I did some fast travel on Peepeye today. We might as well camp a little early so he can rest and graze. Won't cost me any time if we dig after dark. You want to camp together tonight?"

"I don't figure anybody will see us out here, son. Be a pleasure to have company." Pa stood rubbing his hands idly on his trousers for a moment before he asked, "How did you decide to start shooting so quick?"

"Their trail came in from one side. They turned and followed your tracks like hounds after a deer. I saw one of them leaning from the saddle to do the trailing, so I had no doubt. Besides, nobody travels at that pace unless he's trying to run somebody down. When I circled to get ahead of them, thinking to spring my own ambush, I had to push Peepeye hard. But when I came around, I saw them ride up. They saw your horses and stopped. They pulled rifles and dismounted. They knelt down and had rifles shouldered and ready to shoot if you came in sight. Guilty. Death sentence. Next case."

Pa nodded and turned away. They spelled each other with the shovel, and the soft ground made for easy digging. Both men went into one grave. Neither had to be moved more than five feet from where he fell. Pa insisted on searching both bodies thoroughly, but he found nothing to identify either man. Ward stood quietly, hat in hand, while his father read briefly from the Book.

Ward searched the men's saddlebags and

found no identification or anything he judged worth keeping. He stripped the saddles off their horses and turned them loose. Both men had carried rifles, but Ward had no use for them, so he drove both barrels into the grave mounds and dropped the saddles beside them. They would serve as crude headstones for two nameless, inept outlaws.

After a light meal, and with the sparse fire doused, they sat sipping coffee in the darkness. Pa said simply, "I worry about you shooting somebody by mistake someday, son. A man shouldn't kill unless he's forced to it. It would burden your conscience if an innocent fell."

"I know, Pa."

Later, when they were both in their blankets under a sky blazing with stars, Pa spoke again, "That was nice, fast shooting, son."

"Thank you, sir."

"A good rifle like Nadine deserves to be looked after."

Ward lay staring at the stars for a long time, stung by the softly spoken reprimand. Finally, without another word, he rolled out of his blankets and ran an oiled patch through Nadine's barrel. His Pa had gently shamed him. He should have tended to Nadine before he ever laid hand on that damn shovel to help bury human garbage.

Back in his blankets, Ward felt as though a hand around his heart had tightened. Pa's advice lay heavy on his mind. The truth couldn't be denied. He, even in his fear for Stitch and his anger at the men who took him, had no right to behave like a savage. The freedom from restraint he'd felt for a few days had come from an overheated mind. He had no right to inflict pain on people just because they didn't share his own sense of urgency. A man had no right to expect other people to see or understand his own pain.

People spoke of him as a cold-blooded killer, and Ward had never let himself care what others thought, but he began to see the truth of their talk. He didn't bother to deny, even to himself, that killing hadn't bothered him since the gut-wrenching sickness that followed his first gun-fight.

Something froze inside him that awful day when he'd killed three men almost on the doorstep of the house he'd been born in. That gunfight the evening following his mother's death had been too much for him. Something tender inside him had been injured, and the scar over that tender place must have formed too thick. Since that day, anybody who threatened his kin became a dangerous enemy, too perilous to be tolerated.

Ward dimly remembered reading somewhere about men in India who grabbed up spindly spears and tried to fight off tigers who came into their village at night. He understood them. A man had no worth if he didn't stand between his family and danger, even if all he had were sticks and stones and fingernails.

Ward saw men who threatened his kinfolk to be exactly like tigers. Grieving at their deaths fell beyond absurd; it was fake, the act of a lying fraud. Still, if he got Stitch back, and he couldn't bear to think he might fail in that, he was a father. He had a responsibility as a parent. He couldn't act like a monster with no regrets about killing people.

Ward sat up in shock. He'd just admitted to himself that he was a monster. He pulled his blanket around his shoulders and stared into the night. He didn't feel like a monster, but why should he? Monsters were only monsters in the eyes of others, never in their own view. Thus, if other men and women saw him as a monster, he had to accept it as truth.

Ward felt that every boy had a right to a father he could be proud of. He knew this wasn't true for every boy, but to be able to take pride in one's father was a blessing. Ward had such a father, a godsend to him all the days of his life. He had to learn to do better for his own son. He had to act, to pretend to feel remorse when he did not. He must never let his son know the truth. He would have to live a lie. Pa cleared his throat, and Ward realized his father lay awake, watching him.

"Troubled, son?"

Ward answered without hesitation. At least, with this man, he'd never lie. "Pa, why can I kill people and it doesn't bother me? People expect it to bother me. I know they do. Why am I different?"

Pa's answer came after such a long pause Ward thought he'd drifted off to sleep. "It's because you're my son, Ward."

"Sir?"

"You were born like you are because you're my son. You got no cause to burden yourself with blame. Nobody has ever picked his father, not since the beginning of time."

"You mean it doesn't bother you either, Pa?"

"No." Pa sat up and lifted his blankets to form a hood over his head. His face lay in darkness, shadowed from the light of the rising moon. He sat without speaking for what seemed an eternity, yet Ward knew to keep quiet and wait. Pa often spoke with agonizing slowness when he had something important to say.

"Only Luke avoided the blood stain. He's killed, true, but it breaks his heart. He suffers afterward. He lives in pure torment for a long time. You, Milt, and I carry the stain. We don't care. If it's necessary, we do it. Our only salvation is that we've none of us ever killed anybody who didn't deserve it. But when it happens, when we kill, we don't care. We don't agonize over it later like others do."

"Why? I just sat up like I'd been stung. You know why? I was thinking, and it came to me that I'm a monster, Pa. It kind of jerked me up. I'm sorry if I woke you."

"How many times have you hit your your wife, son?"

"Pa! I never! How could you ask such a thing?"

"How many times have you hit your son?"

"I couldn't hit my boy. No cause for that. He's just a little baby."

Pa chuckled. "He's a hellion, like every other child his age in the world."

"No, no, Pa. He's just got a lot of energy. He's curious and gets into things. He's—"

Pa interrupted. "He's a little hellion. How many times have you ever whipped a horse?"

Ward drew his blankets tighter around himself. A chill had come into the night air. "You're telling me something, but I'm not hearing, am I?"

"Not yet, son, but maybe you'll catch the drift before I'm finished. If you're a monster, you're a special kind. You never show signs of hateful meanness."

Pa drew a deep breath and sighed before he spoke again. "You're born from me, but that's only part of it. If I'd been able to live in a settled town, with law around the corner, you'd not have faced what you have. You've lived rough, had men come at you. You started on the rough road too young. All you can do now is be careful. You've got to be dead right every time you pull a gun. I saw to it that you're good with guns. You have always been careful about who you shoot at, so you think you don't care when they fall. But I've seen men who think they don't care go to pieces if they shoot an innocent. That's what you have to watch out for."

"That's what you meant earlier when you said

it would burden my conscience if an innocent fell?"

Pa dropped the blanket to his shoulders. His unhooded face looked strained and haggard in the moonlight. He lifted a hand and pointed at Ward. Almost like he spoke to inflict a curse, his voice came hard and brittle. "Ward, I'll tell you what I think. You need to hear it because you're on a trail now where the worst might happen. I think if you ever kill an innocent, you'll die from it. You don't mind killing if you feel righteous. Otherwise, it'll destroy you."

The accusing hand dropped. Ward sat transfixed, unable to move, afraid to speak. The silence stretched, near perfect stillness, as if all the creatures of the woods feared and froze, and even the wind held its breath.

Pa's voice held its hard, unyielding tone when he continued. "I think you're weak, Ward, I don't think you've got the power to forgive yourself. That's why men who don't know you think you're fearless. When you fight, you always feel trapped. You don't have real courage. All you have is desperation. That's because you fear yourself more than you fear death. If you don't kill that man facing you, if you turn away and let him live, and if he hurts somebody you love, you'll take the fault for it. You'll kill yourself more painfully than he can. You'll kill yourself an inch at a time, torture yourself to death. You'll do the same thing if you ever kill an innocent. You got to feel righteous in it, or your conscience will kill you."

"Sounds like you're calling me a coward, Pa."

"Maybe I am, son, a peculiar sort of one. I'm telling you, you carry a family weakness. You're a Baynes, so you carry the stain."

Ward chuckled, and Pa leaned forward to demand, "What's funny about that?"

"It just came to me, Pa. I'd rather be a little weak than be a monster."

Pa eased himself back to the ground and pulled his blankets this way and that way until he groaned with comfort. His voice came out pleasant and sleepy. "Set your mind to it, Ward. You have no choice since it was born in you. You're both. One causes the other."

"You've been mighty slow telling me all this, Pa."

"Two reasons. First, I hoped I'd never have to. I hoped you'd have a chance to live peacefully with a good wife, that your gunning days had passed. No such luck. Here we are on this grim trail, hunting bad men. In a settled town with good law, nobody would ever notice you, and you'd never harm anyone, never even know about the monster in you. Second, you've been mighty slow growing up enough to hear it. Some loads aren't fair to put on a boy's shoulders. They're hard enough for a man to bear. Enough talk. Go to sleep."

"Pa."

"Yeah."

"I think you might be getting weird in your old age."

"I'm a Baynes. I was born weird. But I was a good stud in my day. I bred true. All my get is weird too. Go to sleep, Kid Baynes, fearless gunfighter." Pa's derisive chuckle would have wounded the pride of an unknowing man.

Ward made no such mistake. As he lay staring at the stars, he understood what his father had done to him with this brief, almost nonsensical talk, bordering on insult. A thread of restraint had been skillfully woven into Ward's coat. Pa had taken a big part of the responsibility if Ward let himself go, let himself give in to wild blood lust. A blood stain he'd called it. He'd left it for Ward to see it as a stain on the honor of the whole family.

The thought of embarrassing his father, of calling down shame on him, was simply too ugly for a Baynes boy to bear. Strong, lifelong habit ruled the sons of Darnell Baynes, and the old man well knew it. Admiration for him went deep into the bones of his sons, born of his respect for them.

Ward knew he had received a warning, that he faced a test that would determine whether he could hold his father's respect. He faced the possible loss of an asset he'd treasured all his life, without ever realizing what it meant to him. Some things of the greatest value were taken for granted, he realized.

Ward smiled at the bright night sky. His coat had grown heavier with that single thread, a lot heavier. Darnell Baynes might weave slowly, but his skill aroused admiration and wonder. He vowed to remember these tricks his father used to guide his headstrong sons without smothering them. He prayed that he might use them someday on Stitch.

# TEN

TWO DAY'S RIDE SOUTHEAST OF SACRAMENTO,
CALIFORNIA
NOVEMBER 6, 1870

Luke pushed his horse hard, leaning from the saddle to look at the ground. Several times he reined to a halt and stared at the tracks. The second time he dismounted to take a closer look, Cotton dismounted beside him and put a hand on his arm.

He whispered. "Rube, I know you don't like for me to talk to you while we're riding, but you act like something's wrong. What's the matter?"

Luke made a vague gesture toward the line of tracks. "I forgot you're a city boy. The story lies right there. Two men are trailing Pa. Ward's pressing to catch up. Why would anybody trail Pa?"

Cotton asked, "Can you tell how far we're behind?"

"The tracks were made last night. Ward

pushed hard. Looks like he was trying to catch up fast. Look how Peepeye's tracks get much farther apart. He pulled way ahead of us. We better make tracks ourselves. If they had trouble, they got far enough ahead we didn't hear a thing."

Luke settled into a killing pace, but several times he slid from the saddle to jog along the trail. He figured Cotton had brains enough to know he ran in order to see the tracks better than he could from the saddle. Besides, this was no time to waste breath explaining every little thing. Once, sweat streaming down his face and darkening his shirt, he looked up to find a round-eyed look of wonder on Cotton's narrow face.

That expression held no surprise for Luke. Men often seemed shocked to observe the ease a Baynes showed when covering ground on foot. Unlike most horsemen, the members of the Baynes clan ran and walked great distances without discomfort. Louisiana bayous bred good walkers and runners. Horses didn't take to travel in a pirogue or flat-bottomed boat, men were often required to travel on foot and carry heavy loads once they came to relatively solid ground.

When he stopped so suddenly his horse bumped him from behind, Luke looked up to find Cotton pulling his rifle. Luke raised an arm to point at the prints leading off to the left. "Ward cut off yonder way. I'm going to stay on Pa's trail. Cotton, you stay here till I get ahead of you. Keep me in sight, but I want you to hold back a little distance. You bring the horses. I don't want to get caught in the saddle. If I fall into trouble, you'll have room to move free. No need for both of us to fall into the same trap."

Cotton nodded without comment, and Luke moved forward at a fast walk. Cotton might be a city boy, but Luke knew how steady his wife's brother stood under fire. With Cotton behind him, at least he had no worries about guarding his back.

He froze at the sight of fresh earth, an unmistakable grave mound. He forced himself to scan the surrounding woods for an unbearable few minutes before he approached. Dread tightened every muscle in his body. Two rifles and two saddles marked the grave, and Luke stood for a moment sick with doubt.

Neither rifles nor saddles looked familiar, but that didn't carry a sure message that his father and brother might not be underneath that mound. The buzz of flies caught his attention, and he found two black patches in the thin grass. He knew blood when he saw it, no mystery there, but his jaw tightened with anxiety. Whose blood?

Luke circled and finally found clear tracks in a patch of the freshly dug soft ground near the grave mound. He sucked in a deep breath and sighed with relief. Both Ward's small track and Pa's flat-heeled boot showed clearly. Both his kinsmen had walked here after the filling of the grave.

Cotton came forward at Luke's wave. When he arrived, Luke said, "I think everything is all right, but I'm not dead sure yet. I'm going to cross this clearing. Cover me."

Without a word, Cotton dismounted, tied the horses, and moved to behind a tree at the edge of the grassy clearing. Luke broke into a dodging run. On the far side, he dropped to the ground, shifted his position a couple of rolls to the left, and fought for breath. Only a fool stayed in the same place after going to ground. Sweat streamed into his eyes, but he lay still, looking for any sign of movement. Luke could go at his own pace all day without tiring, but he hated running in dashes. He was built for distance, not speed.

He rose to a crouch and moved forward. In less than five minutes, he found the campsite at the edge of the woods. He stepped out and waved Cotton forward. Cotton mounted and rode across the open space. He remained in the saddle, watching, while Luke stood beside the small burned spot of the old camp fire and slowly turned, a few inches at a time, to scan the area.

"Ah! There you are." Luke walked quickly to a nearby tree.

"What? What do you see, Rube?"

Luke stopped and pointed. "See those little notches in that tree?"

Cotton swung down and came to Luke's side. "Where?"

Luke stepped forward to the tree and rubbed his finger along five notches, each about an inch long and an inch apart, cut just deep enough to expose the light underbark. At Cotton's nod,

Luke ran a finger along each notch and raised his hand, fingers spread. Cotton nodded again. Luke stood with his back to the marks on the tree, took five steps and looked down.

Cotton said, "I don't see a damn thing, Rube."

Luke knelt and looked closely at the ground. He rubbed a hand across his face and slung sweat away with a swift, impatient gesture. "Me neither." He went back to the tree and retraced his steps. This time, he knelt and grabbed a handful of grass where he'd last stepped. After four or five tries, a chunk of turf came up with his hand. "Ah! Here we are." He dug a small scrap of paper from the shallow hole.

He looked up at Cotton and grinned. At that moment, Luke didn't care if he looked like a possum eating green persimmons. A flood of relief surged through him, and he noticed for the first time that it was a fine day, a beautiful day. He opened the folded note and read out loud.

"Simple road bandits. Man following me saw them ready themselves to shoot me. You know how he is. Both buried yonder. One lived long enough to talk. No doubt."

Luke glanced up and saw Cotton wearing a grin as relieved as his own. "Any questions, lawyer?"

"No questions, your honor. The court record is brief but clear. Looks like we missed out on the fastest trial, sentence, and execution in history. I wish I'd been here to see it."

Luke said, "Unusual case."

"How so?"

"My pa, the briefest court reporter in the world, says one of those men lived long enough to talk."

"That's unusual?"

"It is for Ward."

Cotton nodded. "I've heard the talk. I have a confession to make, Rube. Ward seems so quiet and shy, I thought all the talk was big smoke but small fire. Guess I was wrong."

Luke swung his head toward the grave and said, "Dead wrong, counselor. Those two make number twelve and thirteen for Ward, if my memory serves." When Cotton's brows rose, Luke added, "Not counting Indians."

Two hours later when they stopped, made a fire, and had water heating for coffee, Luke added, "You know how gunfights mostly go, with people shooting all over the place, reloading and going after it some more?"

Cotton glanced Luke's way and said, "Yeah, it takes a lot of practice to hit anything with a pistol, even when nobody's shooting back."

"Well, I never saw Ward miss in a showdown. I never saw him shoot at a man and miss. You believe that?"

"I do if you tell me so, Rube. Why does it give me a funny feeling in the stomach to hear it?"

Luke dropped a handful of coffee in the boiling water and set the pot off the fire. "Well, I don't know about your stomach, but since I've got you in a believing mood, I'll tell you another thing about my little brother."

"All right, tell me. I'll believe it."

"Ward's the least dangerous man I've ever known, if he's left alone."

Cotton didn't wait for Luke to settle the grounds. He poured coffee into his cup and blew across the top. "I take it back. I don't believe that." He took a cautious sip and sat smiling at Luke for a moment. He touched his lip and stared for a moment at the speck of coffee grounds on his finger. "Why does coffee taste so good with little chewies in it?" He licked his finger to rescue the speck.

SIXTY MILES EAST OF YUMA,
  ARIZONA TERRITORY
NOVEMBER 14, 1870

The stagecoach driver squinted up at Milt. "Happens all the time. We got a rock slide on the road up yonder, and we already got one broken wheel. You men just make yourselves comfortable for a couple of days."

Milt said, "I thought you boys had to get the mail through no matter what."

The driver glanced at the mixture of sweat and dust on his hand, and rubbed it on his pant's leg. "Yeah, our man will take that on through to Yuma on a couple of mules."

"You got any horses we could rent or buy? We'd like to go along." Milt tilted a thumb toward Winston Mill. "Me and my partner are in a hurry."

"Nope."

The man had already begun to turn away when Win's motion caught his eye. Idly, Win polished a half-eagle on his shirt. He balanced the shining coin on the pad of an extended index finger. He stood with his back to two other passengers who traded a gourd back and forth at the water barrel beside the stage station.

The driver glanced around and stuck a hand below the coin. Win tipped his finger and allowed the coin to fall. The driver rubbed his pants again, and the coin disappeared. "Ain't never had nobody ask to get ahead of the stage. Folks always been willing to wait. Don't know no rule against it. Hell, you got a ticket to Yuma anyhow. We got no horses, just mules." He cocked an eye in question.

Milt asked, "Those mules saddle broken?"

"Pack animals. Some have been under a saddle. A good rider won't have no trouble." At Milt's nod, the driver went on. "If you men drop off the mules when you get to Yuma, I don't think there'll be no big disquietude."

Milt nodded. "We'll be ready when your rider is."

While they walked toward the stage, Win spoke in a low tone. "We haven't had a chance for a private word since we left El Paso. The telegram you showed me when you picked it up at El Paso just said they were riding south. How are you going to meet up with your brother?"

"I'll need luck to find him. I'll need luck to get there in time. I got no chance to be lucky unless I work at it."

Win smiled up at Milt. "You'd have made a good cavalry officer. I spent four years in the war riding like hell hoping I didn't get lost and hoping I'd get somewhere in time. We'll make it."

Milt put his hand on Win's shoulder. He knew he didn't need to say anything, but he had to show Win somehow that having a partner like him lifted some of the load. A single encouraging word at times can keep a man from sliding into a black mood.

By the time Win and Milt pitched their saddles down from the top of the Concord and walked to the corral, the mail rider stood holding three mules.

The young rider stuck out a hand and said, "I'm Bates. I got each of you an animal to ride and one to pack your baggage."

Milt took his hand and said, "Baynes." He nodded toward Win and said, "Mill."

Win shook hands and said, "Howdy."

Milt pitched his saddle on one of the mules and said, "Good-looking stock."

Bates nodded and turned toward his mount. Milt had heard these mail riders were supposed to be eighteen years old. If so, this youngster must have lied. He probably weighed in at about a hundred and ten pounds and still waited for his sixteenth birthday. He had one pistol holstered and another stuck under his belt. A Spencer stuck from a boot on his saddle.

Milt asked, "You expect trouble?"

Bates swung into the saddle. "No, sir. The Indians in this part of the country don't bother us on this road. We just got to be sure to stay on the road. Everybody else knows the stage rule not to carry money, so nobody bothers me."

"Am I going to have to dust off this animal to stay in the saddle?"

"No, sir, not more than usual with half-broke stock. Those animals have been under saddles before. I'd watch my seat for the first few miles. After that you'll be all right."

When all three were mounted, Bates spoke again. "Indians give me a look from time to time, but I think they're just having fun. These here are big, fast mules, Mr. Baynes, damn good stock they tell me comes all the way from Missouri. I usually just take out if I see Indians. Their horses ain't too good, and these mules are grain fed. Besides, they got no use for this here mail, and I ain't never seen an Indian would stoop to riding a mule."

At Win's raised brow, Milt commented as they rode at a fast trot away from the stage station, "Some Indians see mules as a freak of nature. I guess they'd call a mule an abomination if they knew the word."

Bates said, "They told me you men have to stay with me all the way. I got to see to it those mules get to Yuma."

Milt nodded. "We'll cause no trouble."

"They tell you I don't stop to camp?"

"Sixty miles without stopping?"

"Yes, sir. I ain't supposed to stop to eat or make coffee or nothing like that. We'll be in the saddle all night. I got to be there before nine o'clock in the morning. I figured they'd told you."

"Saves me trouble, Mr. Bates."

"How's that, sir?"

"I'm in a huffy. I figured I'd have a hard time talking you into a fast trip."

Milt glanced at Win. The man's face showed rigid lines of fatigue. "You all right, partner?"

Win broke out in a gust of laughter. "I never in all my days thought I'd find a saddle on a mule restful. Milt, when we go back home, I'm not riding in a Concord stage. I'll ride a boat, a train, a horse, or I'll walk, but I'm never putting my poor ruined butt on one of those things again. I feel like my guts have torn loose in several places."

"Yeah, maybe it's been a little rough, Win, but it's been a real pleasure in a way."

"All that pounding on your rear end has addled your brain. You found something to pleasure you?"

"Sure. Where else can you get such wonderful food?"

Win just groaned, but Bates thought that remark was hilarious. The kid laughed and snickered for two or three miles. Milt recognized the kid's enjoyment for what it really was. The boy had a hard, dangerous, lonely job. For this trip at least, he had two heavily armed men along. The kid had a right to feel good.

After four hours of silent riding, Bates said, "I'll bet you seen some wonderful country too."

Win said, "Too dry, too windy, too flat, too rocky, too hot by day, too cold by night. Bad water. Rotten food. Everything I've seen since we came west of central Texas either sticks, stings, or stinks."

Innocently, Milt said, "Seems like I saw you admiring a little Mexican woman in El Paso."

Win had shaken off the set expression of a man fighting exhaustion. Without a second of hesitation, he answered, "Even an empty desert has its flowers." He pointed a finger at Milt with his thumb up like a cocked pistol. "Besides, if you plan to tell my wife about that, don't forget to tell her that little Mexican woman was five or six years old."

"What's your count, Mr. Bates?" Milt asked.

"Six, I think, sir."

"What?" Win sat up straighter in the saddle. "What count?"

Milt said, "Six desert flowers that can bloom whenever a man gets careless."

Bates drew his Spencer from its boot. "I see 'em every now and then when I ride along this road. I think they just want to let us know they're watching. Pull your rifles. I think it's a good idea to let them see we're armed and ready." He kicked his mount into a easy canter. "Let's see if we can outrun 'em."

His own Spencer resting on his hip, barrel pointing skyward, Milt said, "I don't think we'd have seen them so easy if they meant to cause trouble. What do you think, Mr. Bates?"

"They never fussed with me before, Mr. Baynes. We've had a little race like this two or three times, but they never troubled me. They'll have to ride hard to catch us. They can come up on us in a short race, but these mules will wear their ponies out in a long run."

Win looked toward the sun. "Only about an hour of daylight left. Will they attack us after nightfall?"

"If they want us they'll attack us inside the gates of hell." Milt laughed and drew a questioning glance from Win. His blood sang through him with a familiar rhapsody, pounding in his ears like an eager drumbeat. Milt made no effort to conceal his high spirits. A ride like this snapped a man from sleepy, monotonous, humdrum existence into the real thrill of living.

A confident potential enemy in his home territory, possibly showing contempt by revealing himself, a race with Milt mounted on an animal he couldn't trust, an unfamiliar trail ahead, light dying as the day ended, two to one odds or worse, these all called to something deep inside him, raised a heady siren song in his blood.

Milt loved his wife dearly. His fondest wish was to be by her side at this very moment. Yet, he thought with a wolfish smile, he also dearly loved simply raising hell. If he were riding alone on this lonely trail right now, he'd turn, fade into the rocks and brush, and add excitement to the lives of his pursuers. Damn, that would be fun! The world was a simpler and more tantalizing place when a man rode alone.

They rode at a steady canter for an hour, dusk settling in, and then, in near darkness, the six braves appeared in the open. They sat their mounts in almost perfect stillness at the far edge of rifle range. Had they delayed only a few minutes, they would have been lost to view.

Win Mill and young Bates flinched in surprise when the shrill, full-throated ululation burst from Milt. Both turned in their saddles to stare in frozen shock as Milt repeated the chilling scream with his head thrown far back, rifle pumping up and down at the sky. Like puppets on a common string, their heads swung toward the six warriors when their answering cries came in a wild, savage chorus, rifles and bows pumping over their heads.

Win shivered and turned back to Milt. "You scared me out of ten years' growth. I've got goose pimples all over me. Why did you do that?"

Milt laughed and shoved his Spencer into its boot. He slowed his mule to a walk. "Courtesy, white man, simple good manners. You might as well give your mounts a breather, gentlemen."

Bates slowed his mount and turned a pale face to Milt. "You scared me white-headed, too, Mr. Baynes. I hope you're gonna tell us more than that. I never heard such a noise from a man."

"When they showed themselves in the last light, just to sit and watch us pass, they told us we won the race. Or, maybe they told us they took a notion this time to let us pass in peace. My war cry told them, 'I'm not afraid of you.' Their answer said, 'We don't fear you either. Come again the next time you feel brave enough, brother.'"

Win turned to Bates. "Watch it, youngster. This man can pass more wind than a bull on spring grass."

Milt laughed again, lifted his hat, and ran his hand through his hair. "Not this time, gentlemen. A good story is always worth telling, and nothing makes the truth took more shabby than a majestic lie, but this is straight. You men need training in the culture of your neighbors."

Win glanced at Bates again. "When he's talking like this, be sure you stay upwind, Mr. Bates." His gaze came back to Milt. "Speak on, royal master of culture."

With a wide swing of his hat and a bow in the saddle, Milt said, "Indians have more fun than white men. You need to learn from them. Now take this little race we just had. You ignorant white men just feel we got away. That's right, of course, but it's too simple.

"We brought honor to ourselves. We rode through enemy country and got away with it. We did a good thing, a brave thing. Now take those boys we just rode past. They detected us, showed alertness which is a good thing, and chased us out of their country, a brave thing. They brought honor on themselves. They made us run away. Everybody wins. Everybody feels good and has something to brag about."

Win sounded thoughtful. "That kind of makes sense. Are you serious, Milt, no fooling?"

Bates shoved his rifle back into its boot. "I believe it. Nobody could make that up so quick. It makes sense. It means we don't have to worry about Indians no more."

Milt's hand shot up. "Whoa, Mr. Bates, hold your horses. It just means we don't have to worry about those particular six Indians. I fear there are more out here among the rocks and cactus and scorpions."

Win asked, "When did you learn to scream like that? That curdled my blood worse than hearing Rebel yells during the war. You sounded like somebody'd shoved a hot poker in your eye."

Milt replaced his hat, deliberately settling it just right. "Shortly after I married your sister, sir, that yell seemed to come natural to me."

"He talks like this when she's miles away." Win spoke to Bates as if Milt were no longer present. "You ought to see how he acts around her. Worst lap dog you ever saw, crawls on his belly wagging his tail."

Milt nodded sadly. "True, Mr. Bates. She's a demon, has magic power over me. It reaches out even into this barren wasteland. But it weakens with distance. If far enough away, I can speak freely."

The young rider smiled at Milt, his expression almost lost in the increasing darkness. "I heard one of the men at the station say you're one of those Louisiana Bayneses, the ones they call the Baynes clan, but I don't believe it. You couldn't be an outlaw."

Milt looked straight ahead. The fun had turned sour, and his voice carried a bitter edge. "I'm Milton Baynes. I could be an outlaw, but I'm not, nor is any of my family. Anybody who says we're outlaws is a damn liar. Remember that, Mr. Bates."

"Yes, sir." The young man rode in silence for several minutes before he spoke again. "Mr. Baynes?"

"Yeah."

"I meant no offense. Remember, I said I didn't believe it."

"Thanks. I spoke too sharply, didn't I? I beg your pardon. It's a subject that rubs my hair the wrong way. Not your fault."

Milt felt a pleasant sense of appreciation when the young rider deftly changed the subject. "We're ahead of schedule, but the animals have had a good breather. Let's push on."

The conversation had ended for the night.

# ELEVEN

NEAR VALLECITO STAGE STATION, CALIFORNIA
NOVEMBER 16, 1870

Micajah sat and stared at his son for a moment before he moved to dismount. Jole's weight had stretched the rope just enough to let his feet reach the ground without standing on tiptoe, but his legs looked as slack as the rest of him. The boy's head hung on a neck that looked limp as a dead turkey's. He gave no sign of being aware of his father's and brother's arrival.

Micajah dismounted and waited for Arlo to put down the Baynes whelp and come running for his horse. He wasn't worth much, but he did a good job looking after horses. He would tend to the unsaddling and stake out the animals where they could graze. As soon as his feet hit the ground, the Baynes whelp toddled into the shack.

That was a good sign. Micajah caught Fane's eye and ducked his head toward the shack. Fane stepped to the door, glanced in, and nodded. The woman must be inside. If she had tried to run off, Micajah doubted Arlo would stop her. Either she couldn't bring herself to abandon the baby or she had enough sense to know she had almost no chance of getting away on foot.

Micajah stepped forward, lifted the rope from the bucket still sitting a few feet in front of Jole, doubled it, and swung. The doubled end of the wet rope struck Jole's temple with a wicked crack. His whole body jerked with the impact, but no sound came from him other than air sucked between clenched teeth.

"You awake now? I told you to think, not sleep."

"Yeah." Jole's voice hardly came out above a mumble.

"What?"

"Yeah." This time he spoke more distinctly.

"Thirsty?"

"Yeah."

Micajah pointed at the bucket. When Fane lifted a brow, Micajah flipped a hand at Jole. Fane walked to the bucket, lifted it slowly, set his feet, and lofted the contents onto his suspended brother. Jole straightened his knees and groaned. When the noise came from him, his head came up and Micajah saw his eyes widen in alarm, but Micajah didn't swing the rope again.

"A man needs to be given time to ponder things once in a while. You been doing some thinking, son?"

"Yeah."

"You figure out why you're hanging from a tree?"

"Yeah."

"I figure you've been there for about twelve hours. That should be long enough for you to have it all figured out. Tell me why you're hanging from a tree."

"Because of that damn Mex bitch."

Micajah draped the rope over his shoulder, fumbled in his pocket, and pulled out a frayed cigar butt. He licked the ragged smoke and rolled it into a semblance of its original shape, struck a match on his boot sole, and stood staring into the distance, his head wreathed in smoke. Then he deliberately pulled the rope from his shoulder and carefully matched the loose ends together. Jole ducked his head and tried a futile effort to turn away, but all he managed was the feeble, grotesque dance of a trussed puppet on a single vibrating string. Micajah swung the doubled rope wide and whipped it across Jole's chest. A six-inch tear opened above the pocket of his shirt, and red began to spread on the wet garment.

"I can see you ain't thought enough about this here problem, Jole. That was sure enough not a good answer." Micajah turned to Fane. "Take the bucket to the well, fill it, and bring it back."

Fane asked, "How far you going to push this, Paw?"

"As far as I think will do some good. You want to go in the shack with the woman so you don't

130

have to watch? This too much for you?"

"Paw, if we have to ride from here, he ain't going to make it. It'll take him days to get over this if we cut him down right now."

"I ain't sure this one's to be riding with us any-more anyhow."

"You willing to talk about it, Paw?"

"I am if you're willing to fill that bucket like I told you to."

Fane picked up the bucket, filled it, and put it back in its original position a few feet in front of Jole. Arlo came back from staking out the horses, lugging Micajah's saddle. He stood silently look-ing at Jole, tears glistening in his eyes. Micajah rolled the rope into its tight coil and dropped it back into the bucket. He said gently, "Get on with unsaddling Fane's horse now, Arlo."

Arlo dropped the saddle and turned away at once. "Yeah, Paw, I can do that."

Micajah ducked his head toward the shack and Fane followed him inside. The Mex woman had a pot of beans going over a small fire. The shack boasted only a dried mud fireplace and hearth with a thin stack leading to the roof. She wore Jole's shirt and had the whelp perched on her hip. Micajah caught a glimpse of a swollen cheek and puffed lips before her eyes forced him to look away again. He sank to one of the wooden boxes that served for chairs and said, "That's kind of you, little lady. It's been a while since a woman cooked for us."

When she didn't answer, his anger came on

131

him again so hard he heard roaring in his ears. Damn that Jole! He still couldn't meet the woman's eyes because of his thickheaded son. He leaned forward, elbows on his thighs, hands dangling between his legs. He stared at the earth floor until a box creaked when Fane sat down. "You wanted to talk?"

"Paw, I don't think this is going to do no good."

"What's your idea? You got a better way?"

"I hate to see anybody strung up thataway."

"You didn't answer my question, boy." Micajah looked up in time to see Fane's eyes narrow. He made a quick correction, "You didn't answer my question, Fane." The tension eased out of Fane's shoulder, and lines around his mouth formed almost into a smile.

He leaned forward and spoke softly. "I don't think nothing will change him, Paw. I think Jole's always going to be the way he is."

"I was near killing him this morning, son. It was a close thing. You think I got to kill one of my own boys?"

"Paw, it ain't like this is the first time Jole's done this kind of thing. I told you he's as bad as Burl was."

Micajah's head snapped up and he met Fane's eyes for a moment before his head drooped and his gaze centered on the floor between his knees. "Seems like there's a lot I ain't heard about my own family." He heaved a deep sigh. "Fane, I ain't up to hearing no more. I'm fighting the devil's temptation. I'm near set in my mind to go shoot that boy where he hangs, but I know I ain't up to it. I know I'd fold. I'd stand there not up to pulling the trigger."

The Mexican woman put a couple of sticks under the kettle. She hardly made more sound than a bird building its nest in the doing of it. Thin smoke drifted out the door. The tin stack must not be drawing right again. If the wind blew from the wrong direction, half the smoke drifted around inside, making a man's eyes sting. He wiped his face and sat staring down at his cupped hands. "You still didn't answer my question, Fane. What's your idea?"

"Run him off."

Micajah straightened and found himself caught by Fane's unmoving stare. Again, Micajah found he had to look away first. His head dropped, and he spoke to the floor. "You not only grew into a man, Fane. You grew into a hard man, with a heart like a stone."

Fane's hand dropped on his shoulder. "It's not hard, Paw. It's kinder than what you're doing. You got to cut him loose. Nobody can accuse you of not doing your best. You ever heard of a man stringing his own son up to hang all day and beating him with a wet rope? That's no way to treat a man, even a man with the devil in him."

"He'll go off and get into trouble. Somebody'll shoot him or hang him."

"Let them do it, Paw. At least the doing of it won't be on your head. It'll be better than what's happening outside right now. I don't think you needed to have me tell you any more about Jole. It sounds like you knew all along."

"He's your brother."

"He's that, Paw, but that don't make me proud." Fane's hand tightened on Micajah's shoulder. "You had it figured already anyway. You said outside you weren't sure he'd be riding with us anymore."

Micajah nodded, too surprised to try to conceal it. "I did say that, didn't I? I wasn't thinking at all. It just come out of me. If you hadn't reminded me, I would've forgot I said it. Now that's a wonderment, ain't it?"

"There's another thing, Paw. If we get caught doing what we're doing, we might all hang. Jole may be better off riding away from us. Did you think about that?"

Micajah felt his mouth twist. "We're doing him a favor? Is that what you're saying now?"

Fane's gaze didn't waver. "Maybe. I done heard of stranger things."

Micajah stared at the floor, and he realized time had passed in silence when Arlo stepped inside. He edged along the wall, obviously not wanting to bring attention on himself. "Arlo."

"Yeah, Paw."

"Take Jole's saddlebags and saddle over yonder. Go saddle Jole's horse and bring it up here. When you get back, call me."

"I can do that, Paw." He walked fast toward the door.

"Arlo."

"Yeah, Paw." He stopped instantly and turned to face Micajah.

"Tell me what you got to do."

"I saddle Jole's horse and bring it up here. When I get that done I holler for you."

"Don't forget Jole's saddlebags."

"I won't, Paw. I can do that."

At his father's nod, he stepped out the door. His running footsteps came plainly in the silence. Head down and staring at the floor again, Micajah said, "His kind lives close to the angels."

Fane's answer came so low Micajah almost didn't hear it in the quiet room. "I know, Paw."

The room remained so still Micajah could hear his own breathing. A quick glance showed the woman seated in the darkest corner, the baby asleep in her lap. The only light came from the feeble flicker of her meager fire.

"Once I had land, slaves, a loving wife, and four sons. Now I don't own nothing. Wife's gone. One of my sons is dead, and I'm about to drive another away."

The box creaked when Fane shifted his weight, but he said nothing.

"Could you have drawn on me today, Fane?"

"Yeah, Paw."

"You sure?"

"Yeah, Paw, but we're past that now. Don't think no more on it. We reached an understanding. If it troubles your mind, I can ride from here, too, but I ain't riding the same trail with Jole no more."

"I guess I'm getting old."

"Yeah, Paw. I see it coming on you."

"If you rode off with me not getting any younger, who'd look after Arlo one of these days?"

"That's the only reason I ain't rode off before, Paw."

"I see. This here's been a hard day for me. I'm seeing a lot I wasn't ready to see before. Fane, if we get that money, it'll mean a whole new start. We can be in Mexico in less than a day's ride. Suppose they can only come up with half what we asked. We'll still have enough to get us a comfortable place."

"Why'd you give them a month, Pa?"

"Can't nobody gather that much in gold real fast, Fane. That Kid Baynes will have to borrow most of it, I'll bet. Besides, I figured to get me more than one Baynes while I was at it. They'll gather. Count on that."

"You willing to take half?"

"Son, I'm willing to take what they offer, and that's fact, as long as it's not such small money as to give insult."

"You still set on killing a Baynes or two?"

Micajah surprised himself. He found it in him to look up at his son and smile. "Son, you figure a way to take money from a Baynes without killing him. You do that, and I'll sure enough listen to it."

Fane grinned back. "I'll ponder on it, Paw."

Arlo appeared at the door. "I done it, Paw. I saddled Jole's horse and put his saddlebags on it. I got the horse outside, and I come to get you."

Micajah came slowly to his feet and stepped through the door. He put a hand on Arlo's shoulder and said, "You done real good."

Arlo smiled from ear to ear and looked at Fane. "Paw said I done good. You hear that, Fane?"

Micajah walked through the gathering dusk to Jole and squatted in front of him. "You ready to come down from there?"

Jole's head came up. "Yeah, Paw."

"Tell me why you been hanging there."

"Because I tried to get with that Mex bitch."

Micajah shook his head sadly. "That ain't the answer." He rose and turned away.

"Wait, Paw." His voice shook and broke, sobs wracking his bowed body. "Don't walk away. Let me try again."

Micajah turned back and stood looking at Jole for a long pause.

"Please, Paw, give me another chance."

"All right. Why have you been hanging there, son?"

"Because I insulted a nice Mexican lady."

"I suppose you're ready to apologize?"

"Yeah, Paw, I'm ready. I'll apologize. I'm sorry as I can be."

Micajah drew his knife and cut the rope. Jole dropped on his face in a sodden heap, his gasp of pain sounding more like the agonized yelp of a kicked dog. Two more slashes with the sharp blade and Jole's hands and feet were freed. He lay with his face in the mud, gasping, his hands seemingly still frozen together behind him.

"Arlo."

"Yeah, Paw."

"Go in the house and bring me a fresh cigar from my saddlebag."

"Yeah, Paw, I can do that." He raced to the shack and returned seconds later with a cigar cradled in both his hands like a clutch of delicate bird eggs.

Micajah bit off the tip, licked the cigar from end to end, and struck a match. "You ready to apologize now, Jole?"

Between shuddering breaths, Jole gasped, "I don't think I can get up yet, Paw."

"You don't need to get up. Wouldn't be right if you did. You just crawl to the door of the shack. Crawling is best for you, Jole."

The twenty steps to the door of the shack took several minutes. Each inch of progress seemed to come only after two or three moans and whimpers. Micajah looked up once to find that Fane had turned his back to stand staring off into the darkness. Arlo stood with a tortured expression, rubbing his hands together and leaning forward as if to help.

Jole finally lay a step or two from the door. Micajah said, "That's close enough. You can talk to her from there."

"Miss?"

"Don't expect her to answer. She won't talk to the likes of you. You do your apologizing."

"I'm sorry, ma'am. I was wrong. I hope you ain't hurt."

"That's good. Now crawl over to your horse yonder."

"My horse?"

"Yeah. You're leaving."

"I can't go nowhere, Paw. I'm near dying."

"Arlo."

"Yeah, Paw."

"Go get Jole's rifle off his saddle. Let Fane unload it for you. Then you go stick the barrel in the fire. Jole needs inspiration."

"Yeah, Paw, I can do that." Arlo trotted toward Jole's horse.

"Aw, Paw, no!" Jole's voice broke into wracking sobs.

"It's up to you, Jole. You get to that horse yonder and get in the saddle before the barrel gets hot, you'll be fine."

Jole surged to his knees and staggered to his feet, arms hanging uselessly at his sides. He floundered like a hopeless drunk to the side of his horse and stood leaning against the animal, blubbering and spitting, face caked with mud.

"Never mind the rifle, Arlo. Help Jole get in the saddle."

Arlo's weak mind had not softened his muscular body. He lifted Jole into the saddle with gentle hands and no noticeable effort. He wrapped

Jole's limp hands around the reins.

"Where you want me to go, Paw," Jole whimpered.

"Wherever that horse takes you will be a blessing, son. Go far. The farther you go the safer you'll be. If I ever see you again, I'm thinking I'll shoot you on sight."

Jole sat in the saddle sobbing until Fane walked up beside him. One glance at Fane's face, and Jole fell silent. "Good-bye, Jole."

Standing only six feet away, Micajah hardly heard him. Yet, a chill struck deep. With only two quiet words, Fane sounded more threatening than anything he himself had said or done this day. Jole must have felt the same icy scorn, worse than all the insult and pain inflicted by his father. He kicked the horse into movement and rode into the darkness.

Fane turned to Micajah. "The plan is to ambush Kid Baynes on the road to Vallecito. If we just shoot him, we won't know if he's carrying the money until too late. Let's talk that over. Maybe something clever will come to us. We can talk over beans." He walked into the shack without a backward glance.

Micajah stood looking up at the sky. Stars looked so close they could be touched if a man stood just a bit taller. He felt no shorter than he had when dawn arrived this morning, but he knew his place had changed this day. He'd taken a small step down, but that's all it took to come off the top of the hill.

Micajah Trampe no longer rode at the head of this family. Fane would always defer to him. He felt that in his bones. But Fane would make the big decisions from now on. This was the way of life, but Micajah had figured it would come a bit at a time, not in one big jolt. The time had come for the old bull to back away. He knew damn well he'd come close to dying today. A little smile cracked his dry lips. Old bulls didn't always know to back away in time.

# TWELVE

Sacramento, California
November 18, 1870

Helen paced the floor until Kit looked up with a smile and put her sewing aside. "Why don't I get my coat and umbrella. We'll go for a little walk."

"Oh, Kit, you don't have to do that. It's misty and chilly outside. I'm sorry, but it's hard for me to hold still."

"A little fresh air never hurt a healthy woman. Give me a minute. I must run upstairs to tell Papa Joe. He'll want to come along."

"That's not necessary, Kit. It's broad daylight. No one will bother us. Besides, the Pinkerton man's lurking around somewhere close. There's no need to bother your father."

"It's necessary if we plan to step outside the door. We don't want Papa Joe to be mad at us — he can be difficult. Ward said something to Papa Joe when he rode out. Papa Joe says Ward left me in his care. I must respect that."

"I'm making everything inconvenient for everyone. I envy your stoic calm."

Kit stopped short of the door and turned abruptly. "Stoic calm?"

"What else would you call it? I don't know how you do it."

Kit laughed and leaned against the door. "Helen, that's easy. I'll tell you how I do it. I fake it. I can't abide my man being ashamed of me, so I put on a false face and hide behind it. All the women out here do that, else the other women cut them dead."

"For heaven's sake, why?"

Kit walked back and dropped into her rocker. She took a deep breath and tipped herself far back to look up at Helen. "My daddy talked to me for hours after I heard that Ward killed two men in the street one day in Montana. Did you hear me? I said he killed two, not just one.

"I cut Ward dead. I made myself sick brooding about how I had let myself fall hopelessly in love with a killer. I couldn't eat for two days. Papa Joe, I think, came near to spanking me, and I was already a grown woman, eighteen years old. Those men made public threats against the Baynes family and my father, and they made insulting comments about me. They came after Ward and threw insults in his face. The law isn't much help in a lot of places out here. It's a different world than back East. Men like that must be confronted and stopped. Ward did so."

"I know that, but how can you be so calm about it?"

"I'm not. I have to pretend, but it's vital to do it well. Papa Joe says fear is contagious. He says a man can catch it from his wife like a scurrilous disease. Besides, if a man's own wife has no confidence in him, who else will? It seems to me a man has enough doubts about himself without his wife adding to them. Out here a man must keep his word, and he must face danger without flinching, or he might as well be dead. Other men won't even deal with him. Like Papa Joe says, they avoid a weak man as if he had a contagious disease."

"Well, I think it's brutal and uncivilized. There's nothing intelligent about letting a few unguarded words result in men shooting each other."

"Of course it sounds like madness to us. We don't have to depend on each other in battle the way men do. We have different responsibilities. They have ways to test each other. Women rarely fight battles, so such testing seems utterly stupid to us, but men find it vital to pass these tests. That makes men different. They circle around each other sending and receiving signals we often don't even see. They just don't come from the same bolt of cloth we come from, Helen."

"I think you're talking nonsense, trying to calm my silly nerves."

"You don't think men and women look at

everything differently? Want to put it to a test?"

"How?"

"I can think of a hundred ways. For example, what do you think about that terrible scar on Ward's cheek?"

Helen drew herself up in surprise. "It's not terrible, Kit. I think it makes him look more handsome. It's a bit rakish, and . . ." She paused. Her next words came hesitantly. "Luke has one, too, you know. I think it . . ." She stopped speaking and turned away, but Kit had already seen her heightened color.

Helen spoke again, but she kept her face averted. "I've never had a sister, Kit. My mother and father died when I was very young. Cotton raised me, but he never talked about certain things. I find talking about intimate matters, like how I feel about Luke's scar, embarrassing. What does that have to do with anything?"

Kit rocked back and forth with a smile. "Don't feel like you have to share anything that makes you feel uncomfortable, Helen. I would like us to be sisters." She laughed and clapped. "We can call ourselves the sisters of the clan."

"That would be wonderful." Helen turned and spoke with such feeling that Kit felt her own stab of embarrassment and dropped her eyes to her sewing.

"To get back to the little example I wanted to use. We might think a scar like that a flaw on another woman. Men would probably ignore it, if they even bothered to notice, but we women admire a scar on a man. It's a battle scar. We women see it and start to simper, don't we? I do. I love to touch it when my husband's asleep, don't you?"

Kit glanced up to meet Helen's gaze. Helen stood blushing so furiously that her eyes watered, but she didn't look away. She nodded mutely, and Kit had to resist the impulse to jump up and hug her. Her wordless sharing that she too caressed her husband's scarred cheek when he slept represented a major confidence from this demure woman. Kit felt a flush of pleasure to have gained her trust.

"Women love heroes. We just want them to become heroes before we fall in love with them. Then we don't have to go through the agony of worrying about them. We want them to retire from all that hero business as soon as we meet them."

"Maybe so, Kit, but it doesn't matter. That doesn't tell me how you can be so calm about all this."

"I have no choice. I do women's work. Ward does men's work. Getting my baby back and coming home safe is a man's job. If I showed more than minor distress, I'd be implying he's not up to the job. The only way I can help him is to show complete confidence."

Kit leaned forward and looked straight at Helen. "Do you have any idea how good our men are at doing their duty? Do you know what kind of man you married, Helen?"

"I think so, but maybe I don't. Cotton seemed uneasy on the train about me coming with Luke."

"Did he say why?"

"He said I might not like being close enough to see Luke face violence. I saw him in a prizefight once. I was so shocked and horrified I wouldn't even let him ask me to marry him when he tried. Then he left New York and went to Wyoming. I nearly went crazy. That's when I learned I couldn't live without him, Kit. I went to Wyoming after him and begged him to marry me."

Kit rocked for a moment without comment. The walk was forgotten. Then she stretched over the arm of her rocker and picked up her sewing. "I guess we're not going for a walk after all, so I might as well get back to my work."

As soon as she had the cloth arranged to her liking, she looked up and spoke again. "You didn't seem all that flighty in Wyoming when that gang came after Luke. In fact, you did beautifully. Seems to me that was test enough to satisfy anybody. After all, Helen, four men were killed that day, if I recall correctly. Both your husband and your brother were right in the middle of it. I don't want to distress you, but I believe Luke killed two of them."

"It happened and it was over. This looks like it's going to drag on for days and days."

"You carried on a bit at the table when Darnell greeted us and laid out the plan."

"What else could I do? Darnell spoke of introducing Luke to the Pinkerton guards so he wouldn't break their bones. Luke doesn't act like that. He made Luke sound like some kind of thug who goes around attacking people. I found that offensive. How else was I to react?"

Kit giggled and drew a sharp glance from Helen. "Darnell knows exactly how Luke acts. You should, too, my dear, unless you were reared in a convent. I'll tell you how to react to a comment like Darnell made. That's easy. You nod wisely. That's all. Otherwise, you don't even dare to blink."

"You think I should simply accept such insults?"

Kit laughed and threw up her hands. "This conversation is delightful. Of course you accept them, my dear. You accept that your immensely big and strong husband would treat men harshly if he suspected them of evil intentions toward his kinfolk. I can see huge, quiet Luke grabbing skulkers in pairs and cracking their heads together like castanets. Where can you find offense in that? Besides, that wasn't what Darnell really said anyway."

"Oh? Did I hear wrong?"

"No, dear, you just heard the words. You didn't hear the hidden meaning, the man-to-man part."

"All right, what was that part?"

"Darnell was saying, 'Son, you are an alert and very powerful ally. I respect your ability and strength, and I want you to know about these friends so you don't hurt them.' That's what he really said."

"I didn't hear that."

"I did, but I've had more chance to be around these men than you have. Also, my father has worked hard to be my interpreter. I had the same problem at first."

After a short silence, Helen sat down in the rocker facing Kit. She smoothed the dark blue dress that so complimented her sapphire eyes, and her hands fussed at her bright blond hair. Her high color still signaled a hesitant and unsure mood. Kit remembered Luke's open admiration for this woman's sharp mental skills, and she wondered if Helen had ever had a woman with whom she could exchange confidences.

Helen spoke slowly. "I wish my father had lived to teach me about things. I feel better. I don't know why. Maybe I'm so upset because I know I don't understand much. You can be my interpreter."

Helen sat looking down at her folded hands. She continued to speak without looking up. "I want Luke to be proud of me, Kit. I want that more than anything. He deserves a good wife."

Kit nodded, realized that Helen didn't see the gesture, and said, "I love you for that, Helen. I'll help if I can. The worst part is feeling helpless and useless. You did hear them decide who would be the chief on this expedition?"

"Of course. Darnell is the head of the family. He made the plan and did the talking. Joe stays behind to take care of things here."

Kit shook her head. "Courtesy. Respect for the senior chiefs. Darnell made it clear that he and Joe only spoke for Ward at that meeting. Darnell and Joe are the elders, the chiefs with the most dents in their armor, the senior advisors. Ward leads. Ward's the injured member of the clan. This war party doesn't plan to take prisoners. Ward made that correction when Darnell misspoke. Didn't you hear that?"

"How can you be so sure?"

"My dear, when Ward spoke up with a correction, and it went unchallenged, the issue was settled. Otherwise, a big discussion would have erupted. These Baynes men talk everything out in advance. I've seen them vote and then talk some more. They make sure they are all of the same mind before they ride into trouble. Your Luke, bless his clever heart, changed the subject quickly to assure it didn't look like Ward was challenging his father. Have you noticed how careful the Baynes men are not to challenge each other? Dangerous men are most careful about that, so careful it's almost amusing at times, even among kinsmen."

Helen shivered and pulled her shawl higher around her shoulders. "You mean they'll just kill the men who took Stitch?"

Kit looked straight into Helen's eyes. "Ward may surprise me. He's not completely predictable. Still, I don't expect to see him again until the men involved in this are all dead."

Kit lowered her gaze to resume her sewing. "You see, Ward has more at stake than I have, Helen. His ability to protect and defend, his very manhood is at stake. I've lost my son if he fails, but I'll still be a respectable woman. He'll have lost his son, but he'll have lost his self-respect too. Men become very unforgiving toward people who put them in this kind of corner."

"But that's ridiculous. It wasn't Ward's fault any of this happened. You and Ward weren't even at home when those men came and stole Stitch."

Kit didn't reply or look up from her sewing. After a short silence, Helen said, "Maybe I'm beginning to understand. Ridiculous or reasonable makes no difference, does it? The only thing that matters is how Ward feels about it."

Kit looked up with a quick smile before returning her attention to her work. "Now you've got it almost right, Helen. You really are beginning to understand."

"Almost right?"

"You'd have it right if you said the only thing that matters is how Ward and Kit feel about it. You see, Helen, I agree with my husband. I have a vote, but we didn't even need to discuss it. That's very nice in this case, since he'd do what he's doing anyway. Lesson number one if you want a happy life with a Baynes, Helen, is don't try to turn him when he's doing what he feels is his duty. You'll only hurt yourself. You might as well throw yourself in front of an ore car. They simply don't feel they have a choice."

Kit's next glance at Helen met a delighted smile. Helen said, "I knew that. I've been living with Luke long enough to have learned a few things. Isn't it odd that this terrible ordeal has brought us closer together, Kit? I never had the joy of really knowing you before. I've had the most awful feeling of jealousy about you because Luke speaks of you so lovingly. Now I'm beginning to see why."

Kit hated it when tears sprang to her eyes and ran down her face. She hated it even more when her voice trembled. "Let's go to the kitchen and get a butcher knife. We need to cut each other and mix blood the way the Indians do when they declare themselves blood brothers."

Helen sprang from her rocker to kneel beside Kit and put comforting arms around her. "I thought you'd never cry. I'll never tell. I swear I won't."

# THIRTEEN

One Hundred Miles North of Vallecito
   Stage Station, California
November 17, 1870

Ward awoke in a blink. He never drifted slowly to awareness or endured groggy moments upon awakening. The rustles, squeaks, and chatter of forest creatures around him sounded normal, and he lay for a few moments with Jesse in hand moving only his eyes until he was assured that nothing seemed out of the ordinary. A slow movement of his head completed his examination before he threw back his blankets and rose to his knees.

With a quick move, he swung Jesse's belt and holster around his hips and settled his hat. He shrugged into his short coat, cut in the Spanish style, and came to his feet. He shook out his boots and pulled them on. Then he stood still for several moments watching to make sure Peepeye and the packhorse grazed undisturbed.

Peepeye had his ways, and if a stranger were close or anything unusual took place near him, his manner would alert a wise observer. Many riders shunned stallions, finding them too troublesome to tolerate. Long ago, Ward had decided that he'd put up with the trouble in exchange for the heightened alertness.

There had been times he'd doubted his own judgment when Peepeye kicked the stuffing out of some other man's horse or tried to mount a sociable mare in the middle of town. That always caused a ruckus, but Peepeye wasn't an ordinary horse. He could talk, and Ward knew his language.

The air lay heavy and damp, and Ward could smell the fog in the predawn darkness. Today looked like it would be spent shrouded in fog harder to see through than a pounding rain. He flipped the square piece of an old oilskin off the firewood he'd laid by last night, uncorked the slim, delicate medicine bottle from his coat pocket, and shook out a match. The dry kindling, protected from the night dampness by the ragged piece of slicker, took instantly to flame. He folded the scrap into his pocket, put on the pot, and turned away.

By the time he came back with the saddled Peepeye and the loaded packhorse, his water had come to a boil. He took the pot off the fire, dumped in coffee, and rolled his bedroll. With his bedroll tied behind Peepeye's saddle, he poured his cup of coffee and sank to his heels. When he rode with his family, Ward ate breakfast with them. When he rode alone, he never fooled with it and never missed it.

Still, he enjoyed a cup of coffee and some quiet time, with everything ready, before he mounted for a day's ride. Today, riding through this soup, he'd have to leave a little later than usual anyway. With the fog blocking the sun, he couldn't trail Pa with yesterday's ease.

Idly, he ran a hand across his face and considered shaving. To hell with it. He'd shaved yesterday. His face wouldn't start to itch before tomorrow. He'd shave tomorrow. With a sigh, he rose and poured a handful of water from his canteen. He wet his face and dug out his razor.

While he sat waiting for his beard to soften a bit, grimacing with a wet face on a chilly morning, he enjoyed a cold smile at himself. In this weather, with nobody able to see more than twenty feet, Pa might take one of his notions to stop for a little talk. Ward didn't want the aggravation of his father's accusing glance at his unshaven face.

Pa wouldn't say anything. He'd just look, and his expression would make Ward feel like a repulsive derelict. Ward shaved with a few efficient strokes without a mirror, smug with the thought that, like Milt, he had only a light beard. Poor Pa had a fast-growing forest of tree stumps to chop from his face every morning. Luke, the smartest of them all, wore a beard he only had to trim with painless scissors every week or so.

Ward rubbed his shaved face. Sometimes he wished he didn't look like an ambitious fourteen-year-old when he let whiskers grow. He'd let it grow like Luke if it wasn't such an embarrassment. He sighed. Nobody could have it both ways. Either you had hard shaving or you grew a pitiful beard.

He tried to keep his mind wandering on trivial paths, but it never worked for long. The heart-breaking picture of Stitch kept popping into Ward's head. He remembered the way the little fellow came running to him with wide blue eyes and that trusting baby's smile, arms held high in happy appeal to be picked up.

If thoughts of Stitch didn't get him, remembering Kit did. Her trusting expression when she said good-bye crept into his mind. She believed he could do anything. Losing Stitch would break his heart, but telling Kit about it would kill him. Ward sucked air through his teeth — the same whistle of pain a man makes when he smashes his thumb with a hammer — and came to his feet.

He put away his razor, doused the fire with the coffee grounds, and mounted with his half-empty cup still in hand. The best thing he could do was to keep busy. At least if he kept moving, he could feel he was making progress, drawing nearer to Stitch. The light failed to improve much, so he dismounted and walked the trail. Even then, he often had to walk bent over to follow Pa's tracks. Ward welcomed the difficulty. He even welcomed the stiffness that crept into his back from walking in a crouch.

The light brightened a little, enough that he could walk upright and see the tracks. He pulled his watch and looked at the inscription Kit had put on it. He felt his chest swell every time he set eyes on that watch, Kit's gift to him the night she agreed to marry him. She'd been so sure he'd ask her she'd already inscribed the date of their betrothal on the timepiece to have it ready for him.

Kit had her ways. Ward had designed their home, now a pitiful pile of ashes. He'd had a little shock when he looked at his first drawing and compared it to the sketches he'd made after talking to her about it. She'd just reminded him of a few things. Her comments shifted rooms, changed their size, widened the fireplace, moved windows, lengthened the porch. In the end, she boasted to everyone about the house he had designed. Sure he had — with her hand guiding his wrist while he made every mark on the plan.

Ward wondered what kind of man could put a torch to another man's dreams, a family's home. Men came with all kinds of ideas about the way things should be. Ward ignored men who wondered how he could kill so coldly, couldn't make himself honestly give a damn what they thought. If they understood, he didn't need to tell them anything. If they didn't, they wouldn't comprehend if he tried to explain. Yet he wouldn't dream of burning a house, and he couldn't shoot a horse. He couldn't even lie about a horse he was

157

trying to sell. Strange. One could never tell what another man's conscience might allow or forbid.

Thirty minutes after he put his watch back in his pocket he realized that he forgot to check the time. Hell, what difference did it make? He was still wearing a grin at his own foolishness when he smelled smoke and frying bacon.

He stood still for a minute or two. The fog deadened sound, shrouding both the view and the ordinary racket of natural creatures going about their business. Ward couldn't help being reminded of the sudden thunder of ducks launching into flight from the Louisiana bayous in mist like this. They vanished and the beat of their wings, absorbed by the fog, ceased long before the circles left behind in the black water went still again.

Ward felt a touch of surprise at himself. He missed duck hunting all of a sudden. He hadn't hunted ducks since he left Louisiana all those years ago, and until this minute had never given it a thought. The thrill of hearing that peculiar, unique ripping sound of air passing through feathers when ducks cupped their wings to land came back to him. The mist shrouding the land today must have brought it back to his mind. That ripping noise came through the fog before the ducks could be seen, a noise to quicken a hunter's heart. A man learned to shoot quickly in those bayous. The hunter who took time to aim came home carrying nothing but a sheepish grin.

No wind. That fire must be close. The chance

of somebody camped exactly on Pa's trail seemed mighty slim. The odds were that Pa had decided to wait for him just as he'd suspected might happen. The bad thing about it was that he'd have to get so close he could hardly avoid being seen if it wasn't Pa. They'd gone to a box-car-sized load of trouble to avoid being seen by anybody, traveling away from easier routes all this way. Ward considered scouting forward on foot, but the idea of leaving his horse behind didn't appeal to him. He backed up a couple of steps and lifted Nadine from her boot on Peepeye's saddle.

"No need to disturb Nadine."

Ward's attention focused toward the low voice, but he saw nothing but hanging mist. "All right, Pa."

"Thought that had to be you. I came out past the limit of where I could smell my smoke and waited for you. I forgot your nose is better than mine." Pa's broad figure came into sight when he straightened to his full height. He'd been in plain view all the time, simply crouched and still, let-ting the fog cover him. "Let's go ahead and take your horses in. We'll have some coffee, and then you can come back out here to wait for your brother. No need to have him smell smoke and spend an hour stalking like you were getting ready to do."

Horses staked nearby, they squatted on oppo-site sides of the fire and cradled coffee cups. Pa, always quiet in camp, spoke in whispers, pointing at a skillet full of bacon. "You don't have to eat that if you don't want it. I thought you might eat though, since you don't have to stir your lazy bones to cook it."

Ward sat for a moment, letting the quietness settle between them. Finally, he reached a slow hand toward the biscuits half covering a tin plate beside the fire. "I might gather enough strength to chew, given time."

The laugh lines around Pa's mouth deepened. "Don't take too long. You know how Luke is about stray food."

"Yes, sir. He's got a soft heart. He takes it in."

"You all right, son?"

"Yes, sir. I'm fine."

"Good. I like the looks of you. For a few days you had glazed eyes like a feverish man."

"Over that."

"Good. You know, I've always felt the cool man has an edge in time of trouble."

"Pa, the man with the biggest advantage is the man who doesn't give a damn."

"Maybe so, son, but I'd rather bet on the man who's convinced he's right. That kind of man's hard to stop."

Ward ate a soda biscuit stuffed with bacon and found the eating of it stirred his hunger, so he ate another.

"You might leave some for your big brother."

"Hell with him. I never liked him anyway."

Pa chuckled. "If I know him, he had enough breakfast for two or three before he forked a horse this morning. But he gets hollow again in about an hour." His gaze searched the fog for a few minutes before he asked in his sibilant whisper. "What's your feel for Cotton Sands?"

"City boy, but steady and a good shot. Like me, too little to be much good in a brawl. Smart. Main thing is, Luke trusts him. Luke's a good judge." Ward glanced at his father with a grin. "Come to think of it, Luke really is a judge, isn't he? I forget that sometimes."

"We might have use for him."

"Who? Cotton?"

Pa gave Ward a stern look. "No. President Grant."

"What's your thinking, Pa?"

"He's not one of us. If we're up against somebody who knows us on sight, he could give us an edge. He looks soft. He surely doesn't look like a man who carries three pistols. Maybe he could scout ahead and find out something without being suspected of being with us."

"Good thinking. Luke gave him those two derringers he carries hid away under his coat. Have you had a chance to take a look at them, Pa?"

"Yeah. Beautiful. Luke spent some money."

Ward chuckled. "You could say the same thing about that Yankee wife Luke found in New York. Pretty woman. Looks expensive."

Straight faced, Pa answered, "I taught my boys right. They wouldn't dare drag something cheap home with them. She's a mite skittish about guns, but I like her."

After a long pause, Pa looked up with a raised brow. Ward answered the silent question. "I hardly know her. Yankee woman, formal, keeps her distance. I want to like her. Right now I just respect her."

"Why?"

"Brainy woman. The story I got was she tracked him all the way from New York to Wyoming to collect his scalp. Any woman smart enough to chase after Luke must be uncommonly clever."

"That's where she's different from your Kit."

"How's that, Pa?"

"Any woman simple enough to chase after you must be uncommonly slow, especially if she's as pretty as Kit."

"I think I just got insulted for waiting too long to go watch for Luke."

Pa gave his grin with the corners turned down. "I cling to hope for you, son. No matter what happens, I cling to hope."

Ward's grin stayed on his face while he crept through the shroud of fog along Pa's back trail. Pa's conversation ducked and dodged along a crooked path and ended with a playful insult, just the thing to loosen up his youngest son.

Pa's fondness for Kit had been obvious almost from the minute he met her. Kit wore Ward's mother's wedding ring. Nothing could symbolize Pa's affection more dramatically than that gift. But it was Pa's way to remind Ward how much he loved Kit by pretending to insult her intelligence.

And for half an hour, Ward's mind had been distracted from worrying, from thinking about Stitch.

Ward found a comfortable place and settled Nadine in the crook of his arm to wait. After a few minutes, he smelled bacon frying. He moved another hundred yards. Luke had a sharp nose. If he smelled Pa preparing a morsel for him, he might leave the trail and circle, wasting time and energy. Ward settled in and another thought struck him. His patience had come back. The jumpy, nervy, skittish tension had quieted. Now he understood Pa's comment about his eyes losing their feverish cast. He did feel more like his normal self. He played with the idea for a while, surprised at how much he actually did feel newly recovered from a bad fever.

The dull thuds of horses' hooves finally came. Ward came to his feet and waited until the tall figure came into clear sight. "Pa's waiting up ahead." The snap of a cocking rifle came clearly, and Ward found himself looking down the wrong end of a barrel at a range of about twenty yards.

"Whew! Ward, you can scare a man near to death." Cotton's hushed voice had the breathy sound of a startled man.

Luke uncocked his rifle and shoved it into its boot. "He took it easy on us this time, Cotton. He's got a catamount scream he uses sometimes when he creeps up behind people. Now that'll stop a man's heart and start his bowels."

Cotton rode up beside Ward and stuck out a

hand. He said, "Good morning, or afternoon, or evening, or whatever it is." Ward gripped his hand.

"Noon is drawing near," Luke commented.

"How can you tell?" Cotton asked, glancing up at the thick overcast sky.

"Stomach clock," Ward said. "Luke's got the best."

Luke swung down and gripped Ward's shoulders. "Who spoke back there, Nadine or Jesse?"

"Nadine."

Cotton asked, "What are you talking about?"

Luke pointed at the rifle in the crook of Ward's arm. "That's Nadine." His finger moved to indicate the Navy on Ward's hip. "That's Jesse."

"Am I supposed to shake hands, tip my hand, or just mumble howdy?"

"You're supposed to talk in whispers. Pa likes a quiet camp. He's up ahead cooking, knowing Luke's coming along."

They led their horses and followed Ward on foot to the camp. The fire burned cheerfully but unattended, with the skillet set aside.

Ward spoke in a low tone. "Coming in, Pa."

"Come on in, son." Pa appeared, leaned his rifle against a tree, and put the skillet back on the fire. He silently shook hands with the two new arrivals and spoke in his hissing whisper. "You boys don't look too travel worn."

"Easy trip so far." Luke already had a biscuit in hand and a strip of bacon balanced on his knife.

"Help yourself," Pa said, hands on hips, giving Luke his grin with the corners pulled down.

Luke flipped a hand full of biscuit toward Ward. "Boy, look after those horses." Ward picked up the dropped reins of Luke's mount and held out a hand for Cotton's.

Cotton said, "I'll help, Ward."

Ward waved him off and took the reins from his hand. "Little brothers always have to shovel this kind of shit." He heard muffled chuckles behind him while he took the horses to grass.

When he returned, Pa had scrubbed a piece of ground bare. "Now, boys, we're about a hundred miles, I figure, give or take about fifty, from Vallecito Stage Station. The old Butterfield Stage Route goes along about like this." He drew a line with a stick. "We're getting into dry country. Fact is, from Yuma, about here, west to Vallecito, about here, there's no dependable water that I recall. I think that's about a hundred dry miles. The Mexican border runs along about here." He drew another line. "There are marshes around Vallecito. Folks call them *ciénagas* down here. We can find water by digging a few feet down. Lots of mesquite. That's the first green I remember seeing when a man comes from the Yuma side."

He straightened and dropped the stick on the drawing. "That the way you boys remember it?"

Ward and Luke nodded. Cotton stared at the scratches on the ground.

Pa said, "How do you want to handle it, Ward? We're getting close. Nobody has seen us. I'll bet on that. If they expect to have warning before we get close, they won't have it. We still have to have a plan."

Ward took a step forward. "I don't know what they really want. If all they want is to kill me, they'll lay in ambush somewhere along the trail with a rifle. They'll shoot me out of the saddle and ride on. If chased, they can cross into Mexico in less than a day's ride, or they can ride east into Arizona territory and hide out in Indian country."

Ward stopped and glanced around, but no one spoke. They stood waiting for him. "If that's all they want, they've probably already killed Maria and Stitch, having no use for them. I'm praying they want the money. If they do, they may have kept Maria and Stitch alive to pull me in. Even if they want to kill me, they may figure they need those two for bait. All I can hope for is that their greed is bigger than their meanness."

Pa turned to Cotton and said, "If our guess is right about the Trampe family being behind this, we've got them outnumbered unless they have other help. I've been thinking on it. There was Micajah, the father, and four boys. We killed one before we left home, either Jole or Burl. It doesn't make any difference which one it was. They were both poisonous, cowardly boys. Then there was Arlo, a simpleton. Fane, the oldest boy, was quiet and the best of the lot. I think Micajah and Fane are the only ones to worry about unless you turn your back. Anyway, there are only four

166

of them, and the youngest is weak-minded. I never saw poor Arlo touch a gun."

Luke said, "Burl was the one that fell in front of our house in Louisiana, Pa, but you're right. He and Jole were about the same. Unless the years have changed him, Jole will run away from a stand-up fight. Fane's different. Fane's tough and smart." Luke shifted his weight and pulled idly at a button on his shirt.

Ward knew the signs. His big brother wanted to say more, but he always needed to be asked. "Say your piece, Luke."

Luke rubbed his hands on his pants, took a slow breath, and looked away. "I always liked Fane."

"You don't think he's in on this?" Ward asked.

"Years pass, Ward. People change. No telling but what none of the Trampes are in this. It just doesn't seem like Fane's nature, not the way I remember him."

Cotton said, "Judges hate to misjudge people."

Even coming from a family known for its twisted wit, the remark startled Ward. This was no time for levity of any kind. He searched Cotton's face for a trace of humor but found none. The man had made a flat, apparently dumb statement. In that instant, Ward realized how deeply Cotton's affection for Luke went. The man couldn't abide seeing Luke's discomfort, so he made a seemingly nonsensical remark to divert attention from Luke for a moment. Ward never stopped to consider the oddity of how such foolishness could prove more to him than Cotton leaving his home and business to travel all this way. This had more to do with faith than fact.

Ward's hand went to Cotton's shoulder. "Pa, I think the clan just got bigger by one."

Pa, alert and quick as ever, said, "We're never in too big a hurry to miss a chance to celebrate. You've just been adopted, Cotton."

Cotton jerked away and walked to his saddlebags. The Baynes men exchanged surprised glances. Cotton's manner of movement had been stiff, like the walk of an angry man. He pulled a bottle into sight and returned. "I carry this for emergencies." He pulled the cork, poured whiskey into each man's coffee, and raised his tin cup. "To kinship by choice, mankind's greatest honor."

After they touched cups and drank, Cotton said, "As a member of the family, I'd like to put my oar in, if an opinion wouldn't cause offense." He slanted a glance at Ward. When he got an answering nod, he went on, "I don't think Ward should carry the money."

When they waited without comment for him to explain, he said, "If all they want is to shoot Ward, they'll probably try it from ambush, and they may get him. He's got to take his chances to smoke them out. We'll probably only have a chance to get revenge later by running them down. Agreed?"

Eyes fixed on Ward, he waited until he received

another slow nod. "In that case, risking the money makes no sense. If they want the money, they won't know for sure Ward even has it unless they approach him. Right?"

He waited for yet another nod before continuing. "Ward's story, if they approach him somehow other than with gunfire, is that Darnell won't let him have the money unless he can report that the little grandson is alive and well." Cotton tipped his head toward Pa. "Darnell has the money, and Darnell wants to see for himself that he isn't getting rooked. If they don't know it already, that tips our hand that Darnell came with Ward, but if we're lucky and careful, they still won't know the odds are against them. Luke and I can trail behind. Maybe we can come up on them by surprise and do some good."

"Sounds worth trying. What do you think?" Ward's comment freed his kinsmen to vote.

Pa said, "I agree. That might work."

Cotton said, "What about Milt?"

With a grim smile, Ward answered, "Milt's always the wild card. Nobody ever knows when the joker will turn up. At least, in Milt's case, if we draw him, he'll better our hand. If they draw him, he'll damn sure ruin theirs."

Pa said, "Milt, when the notion strikes him, can cover ground fast. We're supposed to have a month. Almost three weeks have passed. We can get there in two or three days. My bet is that Milt's already scouting around closer than we are."

Cotton said softly, "The bad side of the plan is that both Darnell and Ward are in dire risk. It could get both of you killed. Then the only response left for Luke and me will be to track them down and get revenge. That bitter result is entirely possible, gentlemen."

Ward faced his father. "Our only hope is that they want that money in the worst way. If that's true, Pa, then it all hinges on how well we negotiate. We'll have to gamble that their mouths will water so much at the sight of that gold they'll be willing to dicker. If we show the money and stand fast, don't let them disarm us or make us helpless, we'll have a fighting chance. Even if they haul off and shoot us, we'll have a chance to get off our own shots before we go down."

Luke glanced at Cotton. "Ward's always had a cheerful side."

Cotton asked, "Darnell, how do you keep from riding in circles in this fog?"

"Two ways, son. First, I haven't moved a step since this fog dropped on us. That's a good way. Another is, I have a compass."

Cotton answered in the whisper Ward had warned him to use in Pa's camp. "A plan is like a compass. Let's hope ours leads us the right direction."

A hissing chorus came from the Baynes men. In unison they said, "Amen."

"Another thing," Cotton added, "I think Darnell should ride behind Ward now but close enough to keep him in sight. Luke and I will ride behind Darnell but close enough to keep him in view. That way, we have a good chance they might not see us all, but we'll be close enough to react when something happens."

Ward said, "All right."

"And one more thing." Cotton looked all around like he feared the wrong person might hear. He bent forward and the others stepped closer to draw their heads closer to his. "I haven't whispered this much since I was a boy telling dirty jokes in the back row of the schoolhouse."

# FOURTEEN

East of Vallecito Stage Station,
   California
November 16, 1870

Milt sat cross-legged beside the skimpy fire and stared at Win. "I got an idea you might not like, dwarf."

"Don't try to insult me. I'm used to envious comments, had to deal with them all my life. All you overgrown, crude men hate to even look at a quality man like me. That's why I'm short. All the rough makings were left out. All that's left is pure, smooth quality." Win lifted his coffee cup like a delicate china piece, little finger raised. "If you think I might not like your idea, you're probably right. It probably rates middling stupid."

Milt pretended he hadn't heard a word. "I've ridden through this country before. We didn't spend much time in these parts, but I had a chance to snoop around. Vallecito Stage Station, unless they moved it, should be about five miles

172

yonder way." He pointed. "If I remember correctly, and I always do, if you ride straight north from here, you'll hit the stage road. Turn left and you come to the station in a mile or so. Think you'll recognize the stage road when you see it?"

"Let's see now, six-inch-deep ruts about four or five feet apart. I think I might notice it if I'm in one of my sober moments." Win spoke with a straight face, faking wide-eyed sincerity.

"A day's rest sure restored your mouth."

"I feel better. Slept most of the time. I don't see how you do it, Milt. You never get tired. Where did you go while I was sleeping?"

"I rode around and checked where the stage station is, just to be sure I remembered correctly, like I always do. I never have needed as much sleep as other people. I guess it comes from having a clear conscience." Milt leaned forward and extended his cup. Win, sitting closer to the pot, hoisted it from beside the fire and poured.

Settling back in comfort, Milt said, "We're close, Win. It's important that both of us be rested and sharp. My idea is to ride around and scout some old shacks and mines I remember, places where somebody might hole up. I'd rather ride alone." He ducked his head in apology and added, "No offense. It's just a habit that comforts me."

"You want me to sit here and fight boredom? That isn't what I rode myself nearly to death getting here to do, Milt. I admit I was exhausted, but I'm rested now."

"Now don't get yourself in a huff, dwarf. I thought you might ride to Vallecito. Look around. Act like a pilgrim just passing through and all tired out, hanging around like you're resting up. You might pick up something. I'm afraid for you to ask questions. Somebody at Vallecito might be in with the people we want. If we're dealing with the Trampes like Pa suspicioned in his telegram, I figure you might recognize them if any of them come around. I know they'd identify me on sight, and they might be so glad to see me they'd try to kiss me. I'd probably have to go to shooting right off. That might be the worst possible thing, might ruin everything for Ward's baby. Ward would never forgive me."

Win said, "I think I'm getting the vapors. I have a sinking feeling."

Milt's head jerked up. "What's the matter? You feel sick?"

"No. You just came up with an idea that makes sense to me. I must need more rest."

"You like it?"

"We do what each of us does best. You sneak around like a chicken-thieving coyote with sore feet, and I go act like a dumb pilgrim and get myself shot if I make a slip."

"Yeah, you can do a dumb pilgrim act without straining."

"Thanks."

"One word of advice, Win, not meaning to give offense."

"All right."

"Don't look anybody straight in the eye. Nobody will think you're dangerous if you look off to the side a bit. Your eyes are a dead give-away."

Win's mouth went into a sour twist. "All right."

Milt leaned forward and put his hand on Win's arm. "Partner, right this minute I'm talking serious business. Nobody notices you until you look them in the face. When they see your eyes straight on, they see a veteran cavalry officer, a trail boss, a tough hombre. They see a man who gives orders and expects men to jump."

Win snapped his head in a sharp nod. "Noted."

"And don't talk like that. You bark 'noted' at somebody and they'll see that blue uniform on you plain as day."

Win snapped his head in the same sharp nod. "Noted."

Milt jerked his hand away and settled back. "Damn hard-headed Yankee."

"I'm listening. I'm listening. Ease up." Win glanced at Milt and snickered.

Milt's next comment came as if he spoke to himself. "I'd rather scout around at night, but that'd make me too slow. I fear we don't have much time." He looked up at Win. "Rushing around in a hurry can get a man in graveyard trouble."

"Agreed, Milt. Getting yourself killed sends no babies back home. Look to yourself."

Milt rose and flipped the last drops from his cup. "My horse is already saddled. I'll be going."

"I still marvel at how you talked those people out of the best horses in Yuma." Win shook his head. "Those people didn't want to sell. Not one bit."

"Smart." Milt flashed his arrogant grin when Win glanced up. "Those men knew for certain I was willing to pay top price for those horses or steal them. I looked them right in the eye, and they saw the best horse thief west of the Mississippi. The choice was theirs. I'll meet you right here in two days." Without a backward glance, he walked to his horse and rode out.

Milt felt a sense of relief before he'd ridden a hundred yards. He had a fine rifle and pistol with forty rounds for each. Dressed all in leather, carrying two canteens, a pair of expensive binoculars he'd stolen in Goliad, a pouch of jerky, a bag filled with four quarts of corn for his horse, and a single thick wool blanket, he looked forward to doing what he believed himself best at doing, second to no other white man.

Now free of worry about anyone but himself, he savored a scout through what he had to consider enemy ground. Like some Plains Indians, Milt tended to believe in fasting on the warpath. He carried little food, and he often hardly touched what he carried. He didn't even bother to carry coffee. This kind of life offered too much excitement to sit around like a placid cow, chewing and digesting. Besides, building a cooking fire in enemy country was so dangerous as to border on madness.

Ward, Luke, and Pa would be tickled just to get Stitch and the woman back alive and well. Milt chuckled to himself. A better victory would be to find them and steal them out from under the noses of their captors. With the woman and child safe, then the best sport would come from pursuing the bastards. Kill them one at a time. Slit one throat. Wait a couple of days while they ran in terror. Then slit another throat. Cat and mouse. Once the woman and child were out of it, a man could enjoy himself. Business before pleasure.

He came to the head of the narrow draw he'd followed. When he rode farther, he'd be visible to anyone watching from a distance. He slid from the saddle and crawled to the edge of level ground. He settled himself with a happy sigh and spent the next ten or twenty minutes scanning. This couldn't be rushed. One of life's greatest satisfactions lay in seeing but not being seen. The unseen man had power. The hidden man controlled his world, ruled over all those he could observe, could pick the time and place if he chose to act.

Win called him a chicken-thieving coyote. Wonderful. Win, bless his heart, didn't even know he'd made Milt swell with pride. He thought he'd come up with a clever, although teasing, insult. He probably didn't know the Plains Indians regarded the coyote as a winsome, playful trickster among the gods found in nature. Surely, if Milt were an Indian, the coyote would be his medicine spirit.

His next observation point and the route to it selected, he returned to his horse and rose confidently, eyes always busy.

He had to gamble. Pa's telegram said Ward had instructions to come to Vallecito Stage Station. Vallecito meant small valley in Spanish. There might be a dozen places in California called that by local people. He had to pray that the stage station part of the message was accurate. This was the only stage station by that name. Milt felt sure of that. If they wanted to stay hidden, he reasoned, they wouldn't come near the station. Sending Win there was just insurance. If they worked with anyone there, Win would smell it. The slight little red-headed Yankee had acute instincts.

The best chance lay in searching along the stage route heading north and west toward the coast. With Ward coming from the north, they wouldn't plan to intercept him on the route leading past the station and on east to Yuma. It made no sense to expect him to approach from that direction.

They couldn't hide from Milt if they had to watch the road. They wouldn't camp alongside the stage road unless blind-dog stupid, but they couldn't camp very far away either. Thus, if they wanted to keep the road under observation, they had to travel every day from their camp. They might be feeble-minded enough to follow the same route back and forth every day from camp to lookout point. In this sparsely settled country, that kind of regularly used trail would be easy to spot. If they chose to make life easy for him, good. Milt nodded, agreeing with himself that he'd gratefully accept that.

He spent the day enjoying the challenge of watching around himself like a mouse in owl country while minding the ground for tracks at the same time. By the time darkness fell, he calculated he'd covered about ten miles of road while riding thirty. He'd followed half a dozen trails, judged them to be false leads, and resumed his travel paralleling the road. Every false lead cost him valuable time, but rewards slide gently into the hands of patient hard workers. Success seldom comes in a landslide. It accumulates, one pebble at a time.

He enjoyed his own smile at the thought of the men and women so blind and deaf he could inspect their homes and walk away unseen in broad daylight. He'd been tempted once or twice to leave a sign just to mystify them, but disturbing their bovine tranquility held no interest. Twice he'd actually watered his horse at someone's well, carefully replacing the bucket exactly as he'd found it.

He found a shallow box canyon that suited him, but it offered no grass or water. He had no feed bag, so he poured a quart of corn into his hat and held it patiently while his horse crunched his way through it. The same procedure accounted for a canteen of his water. He slapped his hat against his leg a couple of times, plopped it back on his head, rolled into his blanket, and slept.

Milt awoke in darkness, glanced at the stars, and knew he had close to an hour to wait for first light. The stars looked down with their friendly, familiar stare, old friends to a man who rode long and often at night. He stretched in sensuous pleasure, carried his blanket a few steps to a big rock and propped his back against it. He reveled in a huge yawn and a long sigh of pure happiness.

Clean and simple aloneness had to be reserved for the blessed. Unbroken quiet, chilled air as pure as heaven's perfume, and leisurely anticipation of another day to float like a hawk at hunt, these gifts proved that perfection could be reached.

Milt's cheeks tightened with a broad smile. The tame could never comprehend the primitive joy of the wild. The clothed and docile could never imagine the raw, guiltless freedom of the naked savage.

The darkness thinned. He poked a strip of jerky into his cheek like a chew of tobacco. Let it soak awhile. Let his stomach appreciate a little anticipation. Milt waited for daybreak, feeling like a kid waiting for Christmas morning. Today the hawk would spy the rabbit. He felt it. He spread his arms like wings, worked his fingers to test the wind, and imagined a world laid out like a private domain viewed from the crystal clear heights of the heavens.

He sprang to his feet. Today he'd find them. Today his gamble would pay off. He'd cross the road and work his way back, checking the other side. The savage didn't question what he knew or how he knew it, and he made no apologies about "mystical nonsense." The savage listened without shame to the quiet voices from deep in his bones. No tracks, no smoke, no sign yet, but that didn't matter. He slapped on the saddle and whispered, "It's a beautiful day, horse. Let's ride the wind."

Patience rode with him all morning while he investigated trail after trail. The sun crossed over and started down the other side of heaven. Then Milt saw his rabbit. The slumped figure rode in the open, head down, arms crossed in front like he was trying to hold himself together. Milt sat in the saddle with the binoculars to his eyes until his heart slowed.

The powerful lenses brought the rider close, but the bowed head and a wide hat covered the features. Maybe the rabbit had been injured, had fallen ill. If so, good. Natural prey for the hawk need not be fit and healthy. The spirits made things easy sometimes. The rabbit rode straight at Milt, so he put the binoculars away and slowly, gently pulled his rifle. No call to make a sudden movement to upset the quarry. The rabbit lifted a hand, removed his hat, rubbed his forehead on a sleeve, and became a man, a man with a familiar face, although the features seemed odd somehow. Milt's smile came near to splitting his dry lips.

Milt wondered if he'd have to rein aside to avoid a collision. The fool rode unaware until ten yards from where Milt sat relaxed in the saddle. Finally, he looked up, eyes round with surprise, and Milt saw the swollen, bruised temple and the blackened, bloated cheek.

"Hello, Jole. Remember me?"

Trampe's mouth fell open, forming an oval of blank, moronic surprise. Almost immediately the surprise vanished and horror appeared. The fool's mouth never closed. He sucked in air with a quivering gulp, like a man dropped into freezing water. A despairing groan sprang from him and rose to a yelp like a dog kicked from sleep. His hands fluttered like startled birds, pulled the reins, dropped them, reached for his rifle, jerked away, reached back for the reins, then back to the rifle.

"A man could grow a beard waiting for you to decide, Jole. You going to run or fight?"

Trampe shrank in the saddle and stopped fluttering. He sat staring at Milt, trembling like a man with palsy. "I didn't see you. You scared me near to death, jumping up like that all of a sudden."

"Look around, Jole. Nothing but rocks and sand around here. I didn't jump at you. You rode up to me like a man asleep."

"I ain't feeling so good."

"What happened to you?"

Trampe's hand rose to his cheek and his pale face took on color. "I had some trouble."

"Tell me about it."

"Never mind. It weren't nothing."

"Why don't you turn just a mite and come with me, Jole? I got a little camp back yonder on the other side of the road. We could sit and talk about old times."

Trampe straightened in the saddle and finally showed gumption enough to stop shaking. "Obliged, but I better keep riding. I got a long ways to go."

Milt kept his tone quiet and flat. "Jole, just turn your horse and ride slow and careful. Keep your hands where I can see them."

"Why you holding a gun on me, Milt? I ain't done nothing to you. I ain't even seen you for years and years."

"I just feel a craving to hear you talk, Jole. Now let's go before I lose my patience and shoot you just for the fun of it."

Trampe turned his horse.

They rode slowly away from the dropping sun, shadows growing longer in front of them. Trampe stood like a swaying drunk when Milt ordered him to dismount in a gully. Milt pulled the knife from Trampe's belt and lifted the rifle from his saddle boot.

"You sure enough move and look like somebody whipped you good, Jole. You got no handgun?"

"Naw, I just got that there rifle."

"You just sit down and hold still. Get comfortable. I'm going to look around for a few minutes."

Trampe sat with the bowed shoulders of a beaten man while Milt scanned all around with his binoculars. Where one Trampe rode, another might be close by. Milt decided to wait for darkness before riding on to meet Win. The closer a man came to his own camp the more caution he should show. He wanted to take no chance he'd be seen and his direction of travel noted.

Trampe sank to one side and lay on the sand curled with his knees drawn to his chin. At full dark, Milt said, "Let's ride."

When Trampe climbed into the saddle like an aged man, Milt asked, "You want me to tie a line around your neck, just to take away the temptation? I'd hate to have to kill you just because you don't think I could shoot you in the dark. I can see plenty good enough to do that, Jole."

Trampe asked, "Why are you doing this, Milt? Why you acting like this?"

"No more talk out here. We'll talk when we get to camp."

Milt headed off at an angle and changed direction twice. When they came close, he hailed the camp. "Win?"

From the darkness, Win's low voice sounded tense. "Who's with you?"

"I found Jole Trampe. He's riding in front of me."

"I can't see him. You in charge?"

184

"Everything's all right, Win."

"What's your pet name for your wife?"

"Demon."

"Come on in."

Mill dismounted and watched Trampe swing down with his stiff old man movements. "Did you have time to collect firewood?"

"Yeah," Win answered. "Not much."

"We don't need much. I just hate to eat raw meat."

"You bring fresh meat?"

"Yeah, I'm not sure how much we'll have to cook him before he's ready to eat. Win, tend the horses while I watch Jole here. Jole, you build the fire. It's for you anyhow."

"What're you talking about, Milt?"

"Just build the fire. Do it."

The small fire burned briskly by the time Win came back from staking out the horses.

Milt kept his voice jovial. "Take off your boots and pants, Jole."

Win's face showed rigid and drawn in the flickering light. "Milt? What are you up to?"

"You may not like to hang around, Win. Why don't you look to the horses? Sometimes a man screaming spooks them."

"You want me to take my pants off?" Trampe's quivering voice brought a smile to Milt's face. Milt knew it to be the smile Cris hated. She said that smile made him look like an arrogant bastard. She called it his leer of contempt. That smile had made her despise him when they first met.

Milt squatted and laid his rifle beside him. He drew his snickersnee from his legging and tested the edge with his thumb. He well knew how the sight of that slim, narrow, double-edged fighting knife chilled some men. "I got a plan to save time. I'm in a hurry to find out some things you know, Jole. I figure to ask you some questions. If I suspicion you're lying or not telling me the whole story, I plan to strip me a rump steak off your ass, cook it, and eat it. That'll give me some supper and you a chance to think. It'll be good for both of us. Then we'll start all over. How's that sound?"

Win said, "Maybe I ought to go stay with the horses. I think you're right, Milt. They might spook."

Trampe crouched with his arms crossed in front of him as if he already stood without pants to cover him. "No. No. Stay here. Please, mister. Don't let him do this."

"This here is Mr. Winston Mill. Mr. Mill, this is Mr. Jole Trampe. Gentlemen, forgive me. I forgot my manners."

Win said, "Howdy, Mr. Trampe. Well, I might stay as long as he likes the answers. If he doesn't like the answers, I'm gone. I got a sensitive stomach."

"What? What you want from me, Milt?"

"Where you got the woman and the baby hid?"

"What woman and baby?"

Milt didn't move except to touch the blade with his thumb, wearing the face of a man in deep thought. Win edged away, shifted his feet, and looked at Milt. "Milt, give me a holler when I can come back. I'm going upwind. I don't think my stomach can take the smell of that kind of cooking."

Trampe went into a huddled crouch, his eyes jerked back and forth as he desperately searched for help or a place to run. "Oh, maybe you mean that Mex bitch? Is that the one? I didn't figure she'd be important to nobody."

"Don't think so, Jole. That doesn't sound like the same woman at all." Milt sprang forward and swung the fist with the knife in it. Trampe didn't even have time to lift his hands to defend himself. The blow took him squarely in the nose. He spun and dropped on his face. Milt stepped on the back of Trampe's neck, stuck his knife back in his legging and whipped out a short length of rawhide. As soon as he had Trampe's hands tied, he grabbed his feet and dragged him closer to the fire. He pulled his knife again and slit the man's belt. The blade ripped through the waist of his trousers and down the back of one thigh. Another cut on the other side and his pants now lay peeled open like the trapdoor on long underwear.

"Now, you want to try again, Jole?" He pressed the point of his snickersnee to the man's left buttock just enough to depress the skin about half an inch.

"Don't cut me! Don't cut me! Paw got a Mexican lady and a little kid, Milt. I didn't have nothing to do with it."

Milt glanced up and caught Win's nod and grin. The former calvary officer knew the value of knowing who your enemies are. Having a talkative prisoner can change the course of a battle if his information comes in time. That one blurted, sniveling remark took half the mystery and gamble out of this whole search. Milt eased the pressure on his snickersnee.

Once he'd started, Trampe babbled on. "I didn't want no part of it. I tried to stop him, but Paw hung me from a tree and beat me with a wet rope. When I wouldn't change my mind, he run me off. I was running when you got me. None of this is my fault. I ain't done nothing."

"Where they got the woman and the child hid, Jole?"

"Old mine shack, north of the road. It's ten or fifteen miles from here."

"How far from the road?"

"Maybe two miles."

Milt let the silence hold while he did his thinking. If Trampe wasn't lying, Milt had turned back too soon today. They were hidden a few miles beyond the loop he'd ridden. If so, this information narrowed his search. He'd find them tomorrow for sure. In fact, he could ride in close tonight and be practically on top of them when dawn came. But, if he did that, he'd be riding a horse into the ground.

He must have covered over forty miles already today. Maybe Win's horse was still fresh. Leaving Win behind might take some persuasion. Milt couldn't think of any inducement that wouldn't make an enemy of a trusted friend. His wife's brother would suffer wounded pride and would never forgive him.

"Who's there besides your old man, Jole?"

"Fane's there, and Arlo. That's all."

"Are the woman and the baby all right?"

"Yeah. Fane tried to get with that Mexican woman, but Paw stopped him."

Milt pressured the snickersnee gently, just enough for the light of the dying fire to reveal blood start to fill the dent in the skin. "I'm getting hungry, Jole."

"Ow! Don't cut me! Don't do that! What's wrong?"

"Don't try to lie to a couple of liars, Jole. We can smell a lie. You smell that, Win?"

"Awful. Sickening. Smells like hair burning, or maybe feathers." Win sounded disgusted and bored.

Milt flicked the point. A half-inch cut dribbled blood down the side of the tense buttock. Another flick opened a matching cut on the other side. Trampe squirmed and floundered like a newly landed bass. He dug his hips into the ground so hard his head and feet rose, bowing his body into a quaking U.

"Ow! Don't do that no more, Milt. All right. All right. I did it. I didn't think nobody'd care about a damn Mex woman. Paw went crazy. Acted like he thought he was God Almighty. Fane too. Looked at me like I'd shit in his dinner plate. She's just a damn Mex woman. Hell, she ain't the Virgin Mary."

"You hurt that woman, Jole?"

"Naw. Paw came back and stopped me before I done any good. She wasn't hurt none."

"The baby all right, Jole?"

"Sure. Ain't nothing wrong with him. Arlo plays with him all the time. The woman looks after the kid, too, feeds him and all that stuff. At least she's good for something."

Milt wiped his knife on the back of Trampe's trouser leg, came to his feet and slipped the blade back into his legging.

Win cocked his head to the side, and Milt walked a few steps away from the fire with him. "What are you going to do with that disgusting swine?"

Milt rubbed his chin with a finger. "I figured to get the woman and Stitch back first and start cutting throats after. I don't see any reason to put it off for this one."

"You plan to walk up and cut his throat? Just like that? A helpless man?"

Milt shrugged. "You got a better idea? You like hanging better? That's all right. You got a rope?"

Win shook his head and looked back at the prone figure lying beside the fire.

Milt said, "I don't like the idea of shooting him. The sound of a shot carries forever out here. I was worried he'd make a break on the way back here and I'd have to shoot him." He paused and grinned. "Wait a minute. You could stick your pistol in his mouth, Win. Maybe that'd keep the noise down."

"Milt, I'm serious."

"Me too. You want to face Ward and tell him you let one of the men who stole his son go free? Wait, that isn't fair. You hardly know Ward. I forgot that. Take my word for it. You don't want to get to know Ward better under those circumstances."

"There ought to be something we can do other than turning him loose or killing him."

"Man who steals babies? Man who tries to rape decent women? Maybe a man who raped a decent woman for all we know? We're not talking about some stranger, you know. This woman is part of my brother's household. You want me to go back and stick another hole in Jole's butt? No telling what may pop out of his mouth next. Win, we've ridden halfway across the country to do a job. We haven't done it yet. I need to find my nephew and get him to a safe place. This bastard is baggage we don't want to carry."

"There's law in California. We could take him to the law."

Milt's rubbing finger went from his chin to his nose. "You do that. I'll keep on with what I'm doing. I'll get Ward's boy back and the woman too. You take this creature to the law. When I get back to Texas, I'll tell Eva you'll be along in a couple or three months, or maybe four or five. I'll tell her you got to testify in a trial. She'll be thrilled. She'll be so proud she'll probably get light-headed and keel over. She won't get lonesome. She won't have trouble looking after your ranch all by herself."

Win stood in silence for a long pause. Finally, Milt said, "My horse is worn out. Can I take yours? I'd like to go ahead and travel tonight, get closer to my nephew. You can go along and find a lawman without being in a big hurry. Of course, if Jole gets loose and wrings your neck or bashes your head in with a rock, that would be sad."

"I can't be a party to murdering a helpless man." Win's tone carried a mix of stubbornness and sadness.

Milt nodded. "Good man. Stand up for your principles. I wouldn't expect you to do anything to disturb your conscience. I suggest you go untie him. If we're not going to kill him, we got to feed him." Milt turned on his heel and strode back to the fire. He already had bacon sliced and in the frying pan when Win slowly walked out of the darkness. He bent over Trampe and untied his hands.

"Bacon and beans, Mr. Trampe." Milt put the skillet on the fire and looked up just as his rifle came off the ground in the hands of Trampe. He fell to the side, clawing for his revolver when his own rifle blasted across the fire. The concussion launched a spray of sparkling coals all over him. The lighter crack of his revolver came a blink later, and Trampe pitched over backward.

Milt lurched to his feet and brushed the

sprinkle of hot sparks from his clothing. When he looked up, he found Win standing like a post, pistol in hand, staring down the barrel at Trampe's body.

Milt glanced at the skillet and said, "I'll bet we got ashes in our bacon."

Win slowly relaxed, uncocked his weapon, and said, "I don't think I'm hungry."

# FIFTEEN

Ward waited impatiently for someone to shoot at him. His desire to shoot back had reached such a fevered pitch that he waited for the slam of a bullet with cheerful anticipation.

He stood in the stirrups for a moment as his eyes moved constantly to scan his flanks. With Pa riding behind, he never bothered to look back. If observed, he wanted to give no easy clue, create no suspicion that Pa followed close behind, that he had his back covered.

Ward sank down and rode, placid and composed in the saddle. He'd never felt so relaxed and yet so alert in all his days. Somehow, when he reached a peak of rage or fear, something perverse in his nature took over, and his life became serene. If this meant he was mad, he welcomed insanity. Maybe God, knowing his weakness, felt pity and loosened the ropes tearing at his frail spirit.

All kinds of madness floated around in the world. Perhaps Ward's brand of lunacy came as a heavenly blessing to soften his last moments. Smiling, he figured he'd never have discerned this about himself without Kit throwing it in his face.

A man can never see himself as clearly as others can. And if that was true, Ward Baynes must be something special for a woman like Kit to take an interest in him. Maybe a man faced death easier if he felt better about himself as he neared the end. Whatever the cause, Ward sucked in a deep breath of the chilled, dry air and considered this to be a perfect day to die.

Ward pulled off his glove and stroked the muscular neck of his boyhood friend. "Peepeye, you should have shopped around and found a more peaceful man. They could shoot at me and hit you. Did you ever think about that?" Pricked ears twitched. Ward had heard men say horses were too dumb to recognize their names. This one sure seemed to prove them wrong. "On the other hand, Peepeye, look at all the fun and excitement you'd have missed."

When the sun shrank his shadow under him, he pulled Peepeye to a halt, checked his watch, and dismounted. Pa said not to try to make time. Ward had no problem with dawdling along. If an observer watched from a distance, nothing was to be gained by making himself hard to catch.

195

Everybody should try to take everything nice and easy today. Pa said each move today would resemble the actions of a couple of warring tribes approaching a peace parley. Everybody should walk on eggs.

Besides, if Ward rode too fast, a distant observer swinging in behind to overtake him might run into Pa. But there was nothing particularly worrisome about that. Pa could take care of himself, but he wanted Ward to do any dickering needed. He wanted Ward to carry the responsibility if anything went wrong. Pa had always been a fair man. Ward had the most to gain, the most to lose, and should carry his own load.

Ward ambled back to his packhorse and acted like a man with all the time in the world, a casual, unhurried traveler. He untied one of his bundles of firewood and started a small fire. As soon as his coffee pot started heating, he poured a small amount of corn into each of the feed bags and slipped them onto his horses. "No big feast, boys. Just a little snack for lunch."

For all he knew, the men he wanted might wait until it was dark to try to contact him. They might want to collect their money and make a safe night ride to Mexico. Another possibility might develop. He might ride all the way to Vallecito Stage Station and find a note waiting for him with who knew what kind of instructions. Pa said to relax and ride with the punches. Good advice, since he had no choice in the matter.

He pulled his knife, slit an opening halfway

round the top of an air-tight of tomatoes, and folded back the lid. Seated, he bit a chunk from a jalapeño pepper and took a swig of tomato juice. Kit always shuddered and grimaced at Ward's Louisiana-bred taste for spicy edibles. Her Virginian tongue couldn't find its way past the burn to enjoy the flavor. She cooked tasteless, bland beans for herself in one pot. Another pot contained his, with a handful of peppers added. She complained his beans made her eyes water if she so much as walked in the kitchen while they cooked. Living with her was just one hell of a lot of fun. He wondered if any other two people could have as much sport and verbal fencing over how beans should be cooked.

He left the empty can conspicuously perched on a big rock. A light riding man can use such gifts left behind by the thinking travelers ahead of him. Everything gathered, he pulled his meager fire apart and mounted.

The Baynes clan had passed through here years ago, but Ward remembered little of the country. Mostly, he had passed through, thinking it pretty but barren. He had little interest in desert and badlands. Any part of the world where a horse could not find good grazing represented a dead loss to his way of thinking. Nobody should bother to live where horses couldn't prosper.

Peepeye eased into a broad gully and Ward heard a call from his left. Nadine leaped from her boot into his hands as he twisted in the saddle and turned Peepeye. A man stood beside his horse only a hundred feet away. He'd picked a perfect place, hidden in a cluster of rocks down in the gully. Had he not stepped into view, Ward knew he could have ridden past him a hundred times without seeing him or his horse.

He walked forward, leading his mount. "Howdy, Ward."

"Hello, Fane."

"I seen somebody way back down the road. That your Pa following behind?"

"Yeah."

"We left word you was to come alone."

"You left word with a man you shot twice. You expect him to get everything right? He nearly bled to death. I'm not sure yet he's going to make it."

"I should just shoot you, leave here, and go shoot that kid of yours."

Looking down the barrel of Trampe's rifle, Ward still held Nadine across his chest. "You could have shot me without calling out. I don't think you're down that low, Fane."

"Not unless you force me to it. You got the money?"

"I don't have that kind of money. My Pa offered to lend it to me, but he won't part with it until he sees the woman and the boy are all right."

"Ward, you might as well drop the rifle and shuck that handgun. You ain't ever going to see that kid if you don't."

"If I don't keep them, you'll never see the money. My Pa and I didn't ride all this way to get robbed. I want to see my son is alive and well. I can't abide the idea of paying you for hurting or killing him."

Trampe stopped walking only about twenty feet away. "I ain't going to tell you again, Ward. You got no choice."

Ward stared straight into the hard eyes looking down sights at him. Trampe stood so close Ward could even tell the man's eyes were blue. "Yeah, I do. I got a choice. So do you. You want the money or not? You shoot me and you lose your chance."

"My paw said you'd drop the guns. I should have known better. Ward, if we ride up with you carrying guns, he'll start shooting."

"Not if you ride ahead. You can ride ahead and talk to him. How did you get into this, Fane? We didn't figure you for this kind of deal."

Trampe shifted his feet and seemed to hesitate for a moment. Then the rifle came down, and he stood with it across his chest. "Your pa should be coming along any minute. You trying to talk so much I go to sleep and forget about him?"

"You know we don't want any shooting until I get my boy and the woman back safe. They are safe, aren't they?"

"Yeah, they're all right."

"Why don't we make an agreement? No shooting until the woman and my son are out of the way."

199

Trampe sneered. "Why should I trust you?"

"Because you know a Baynes keeps his word. That's one reason. Another is, you know it makes sense."

"We'll just wait for your old man and see what he says."

"He should have come along by now. I don't know what's keeping him."

"Circling around takes time, son." Darnell Baynes stepped into sight from almost the same place Fane had. Trampe shifted his feet, glanced over his shoulder, and found himself caught between father and son. "Relax, Fane. I could have shot you dead if I wanted. I never shot a man in the back in my life."

Trampe asked, "How did you get around me so quick?"

"I told Ward to keep himself in sight. He rode down in this gully and didn't come out. That didn't take much thinking, young fellow. I figured he'd run into you, so I circled and did some fast riding."

Fane said, "Well, we figured we'd have to deal with more than one of you. Paw said the Baynes would gather. Any more coming?"

Pa said, "I'm going back down this gully a little ways to collect my horse. You men hold off shooting each other till I get back. I don't want to miss anything."

Ward admired the way Pa changed the subject rather than answer Trampe's question, so he followed his father's lead. "We were just talking about a truce, Pa. I offered not to shoot till we get Maria and Stitch back if they hold off till then too."

Pa's gaze never wavered from Trampe. They stood silently for a moment until Trampe said, "I'd rather get this done without shooting."

"You agree then?" Ward didn't want anything fuzzy about the arrangement.

"All right. No shooting until after. I even got a plan to keep that from happening. We might as well get moving."

Pa nodded. "I'll be back in a minute." He turned and trotted back into the rocks. Neither Ward nor Trampe spoke until Pa came back with his horse at a canter.

Ward still sat as relaxed as ever in the saddle, but now his posture had to be faked. Pa moved fast when needful, and Ward knew the reason for his haste. Pa didn't want to chance Luke and Cotton closing in too soon. He wanted them trailing behind unbeknownst to Trampe.

Trampe mounted and sat looking from one Baynes to the other. Ward said, "We can ride abreast. No need for you to worry, Fane. Our word's good." He wanted to keep Trampe's attention, to keep the man from even thinking about looking back.

Trampe's tone sounded defensive "Mine is, too, but when we get close, I got to holler at Paw. He might take to shooting if I don't holler and let him know you ain't taken me."

They rode for fifteen minutes before Trampe

drew up. "Wait a minute. I ain't seen no gold. Paw'll throw a fit if I don't see gold before we come riding in."

Without halting, Pa unhooked the strap on his saddle bag and dug out the canvas bag. "You can look at it. You can even feel it and bite it. Soon as you're satisfied, hand it back." He stretched and handed the gold over. "That's five hundred gold double eagles."

Trampe's eyes went wide when he felt the weight. He pulled the knot loose and pulled out a couple of the coins. After a quick glance at them, he returned them to the bag and retied it. In answer to Pa's outstretched hand, he handed back the bag.

Pa's straight look never left Trampe's face. "When a Baynes tells you something, Fane, you can take it for gospel. You didn't forget that about us, did you?"

Trampe's eyes dropped. "Damn it, Mr. Baynes, I had to make sure. You would of done the same. This ain't easy for none of us." He put a hand on the pommel and shifted his weight as if readying himself to look back.

Ward said quickly, "Hey, I got an idea."

Trampe's gaze snapped toward him.

"Pa, why don't you give one or two of those coins to Fane. He can show them to his old man. We don't need to go through all of this fumbling around again."

Pa nodded. "Good idea. I won't be turning loose of this bag again until I'm holding my grandson's hand." He went through the motions to untie and reach into the bag again, with Trampe's eyes on him all the time. All three of them had taken to acting like men with painful afflictions, moving with painfully slow care. Again, he stretched to hand over the coins with exaggerated caution. Trampe slipped them into his shirt pocket.

"How far are we from the stage station?" Pa asked.

Trampe answered, "Maybe fifteen miles. We only got a couple of miles to go from here to where Paw's holed up with your folks." Again, he started to shift his weight.

"Why did you come after me, Fane. Why did you burn my house?"

Trampe shook his head. "Paw's had it in his head all these years that we owed you Baynes people a killing to pay for Burl. We were riding through and heard about a Baynes starting to make a name for himself selling good horses. Paw figured that would be somebody from your family. He figured to settle that old blood debt."

He rode in silence for a moment before he continued. "When we rode up, and you weren't there, I think Paw went a little crazy. Losing Burl has been eating at him all these years. He come up with the idea of burning the place and taking the woman and the little boy. Truth to tell, I think we done wrong with that, Ward. Ain't no backing off now though. It's done gone too far."

Pa said, "You still figure we owe you a killing?"

"I talked to Paw about that. There was a lot he didn't know about Burl. He never would listen to me before, but me and him come to a new understanding. I think he's ready to forget about that blood feud. All we want is money. Paw lost everything in the war. All our niggers run off, and all we had left was a little no-account Confederate money. One day a lawman come out and had papers to put us off our land. Paw shot at him and run him off, but neighbors told us he was gathering a posse, so we had to ride."

Trampe fixed his gaze on Ward. "We burned our place before we left. Maybe that's what put it in Paw's mind to fire your place, Ward. When you got nothing, it can grind on a man to see somebody else living high on the hog. That was sure enough a grand house. It don't reflect credit on a man, thinking that way, but I think that might have bothered Paw some."

They rode for a few minutes in silence before Trampe spoke again. "I think I got a plan for us to turn over your folks to you and take the money without any shooting. I sure tried to figure a way."

Ward glanced at his Pa, but his attention was focused on Trampe. Pa had a wrinkled brow, and Ward wondered if his father heard Trampe's talk the same way it sounded to him. Trampe sounded like he was trying to explain, almost apologize.

"If it don't work out, I got a favor to ask."

Pa said, "You're asking us for a favor? Do I hear you right?"

"Yeah. I guess you ain't in no mood for it. Forget it."

Ward said, "Fane, you're trying to tell us something. We don't have much time."

"I don't know how good you remember Arlo."

Ward waited for Pa to answer, but he said nothing. Finally, Ward said, "I remember him."

"You remember how he is, Ward?"

"Yeah."

"Well . . ." Trampe cleared his throat. "Arlo's been kind of lost ever since we left home. He gets lost real easy, you know. He gets confused. We got to watch him everywhere we camp. When he don't have familiar things around, he gets all turned around real easy. You can't let him wander off very far."

Pa said, "We know what you're saying, Fane."

"Thank you, Mr. Baynes. Well, say something don't work out like I got it planned, and we go to shooting at each other. I'd be obliged if you'd remember Arlo don't carry no gun. Arlo don't never touch no guns. He don't understand none of what's happened neither. He just thinks we've got a new baby for him to play with. I don't recollect ever seeing Arlo act so happy. That baby is the best thing that's happened to him since we left Louisiana."

"What's the favor you want?" Ward asked.

"I'd ask you not to shoot at Arlo."

Ward said, "We won't shoot at Arlo, Fane. I promise."

"That's handsome of you. Ward. I'm obliged."

# SIXTEEN

Near Vallecito Stage Station, California
November 18, 1870

Ward felt his stomach tighten at the sight of the miserable little shack. All the planning and riding and agony of the past few weeks had come to a finish. The time to lance the boil had arrived. The next few minutes would determine if the rest of his life had to be lived in sadness. He prayed that today wouldn't mark his greatest failure.

The tall, lanky, bearded figure that appeared in the doorway had a rifle leveled. Fane yelled, "Don't go to shooting, Paw. I made a deal, and they come along just fine. I done give my word there wouldn't be no shooting, Paw. You hear me?"

The rifle lowered and the figure stepped from the shadowed doorway into the slanting afternoon light.

Fane said, "Stop right here."

Ward and Pa pulled their mounts to a halt a

little over a hundred feet from the shack and stayed in the saddle.

Pa raised his voice, "Howdy, Micajah."

Micajah Trampe nodded. "Darnell." He turned his head. "Arlo, get out here and saddle our horses. We'll be leaving shortly."

"I can do that, Paw." Arlo came quickly out the door and trotted toward the small corral behind the shack. He had only gone a few steps when he looked over his shoulder, saw the horsemen, and stopped. He turned back with a broad smile and waved at Ward and Pa.

"Arlo, git on with it."

"I can do that, Paw." He resumed his trot toward the corral.

"Now here's what I got planned." Fane pulled his horse a bit to the side. "We do this one part at a time." He looked at Ward and waited.

Ward said, "Let's hear it."

"We'll ask you to put the gold on the ground. We got us a nice flat place in front of this here shack. After you put down the gold, you back off a good bit, out of good pistol range from the shack, but you can still cover the gold. We'll send out the woman with the boy, and she can come on over to set herself down beside the gold. Paw and Arlo will ride off. When they do that, you can still cover me, your folks, and the gold in good pistol range."

Fane edged his mount a little farther away. Ward saw how carefully he kept himself to the side to keep from being caught between his father and the two Baynes men. Ward's gaze searched for Jole. The shack had no windows in front, and the doorway remained empty. Where the hell was Jole?

As if to show confidence that no shooting would be involved, Fane shoved his own rifle into its boot. "Next, you put your rifles off over yonder. Just walk over yonder a piece and lay them down. I won't be carrying a rifle, so I won't have no advantage. You can still get at the rifles, but not so quick as to get a good shot at me before I can ride off after I get the gold."

Fane rubbed his hands on his shirt and licked dry lips, his first sign of tension. Ward glanced down at his own hands, folded and relaxed on the pommel of his saddle. Fane swallowed and ventured a hard grin. "You got the advantage when I'm standing out there beside the gold by myself. Paw and Arlo will already be moving off, so it'll be the two of you against me. I figure you won't start shooting then for fear of hitting your folks."

He waited as if he expected an answer, so Ward nodded.

"Next, you send me your horses. When I get the horses, I'll walk out there and get our gold. You'll have me under your guns the whole time. No way I can get the gold without carrying my side of the bargain. I'll take your horses with me when I leave. That won't do you no hurt. The stage road's only a couple of miles off. But that'll let us get a good head start before you start a chase should you take the notion."

"Won't take long to run over there and pick up a rifle, Fane." Ward kept his voice reasonable, like his main interest was a fair deal.

"Won't take me long to ride out of sight neither. I got me a direction picked. It's a crooked ride, but I can stay out of sight until I get me some distance. I ain't disposed to be no target."

"Where's Jole, Fane?" Ward kept his voice ordinary, just a man getting the details straight.

"Jole ain't here."

Ward raised a hand slowly and rubbed his mouth. He let the silence speak for him. To speak would risk accusing Fane of lying. Silence would only challenge him to offer proof. The flat around the shack offered no decent place for a man to hide. Ward stared at the shack.

"You think he's hid in there?" Fane's tone struck Ward as mixed. He sounded insulted and embarrassed at the same time. "You can take a look. We'll show our cards. I ain't pulling no trick."

Ward didn't hesitate. He eased Peepeye forward until he came to the sagging hitching rail. Continuing his slow mode of moving, he stepped from the saddle, gave an indifferent glance at Micajah's leveled rifle, and stepped inside. Half expecting to be greeted by shot from a lurking Jole, he couldn't help a quick side step and a drop into a crouch, hand hovering over Jesse.

Maria sat on a box in a dark corner, Stitch on

her lap. She said, "I heard your talk. Jole is not here, *patrón*. The old one beat him with a rope and drove him away."

Stitch saw his father and squealed with delight. He slid from Maria's lap and ran to Ward, arms raised in appeal to be picked up and showing his big smile. He unwittingly matched the picture Ward had carried in his mind through endless tortured days.

"Maria?" Ward's tone carried his concern. He'd just managed to see her face clearly in the dark room. "What've they done?"

Her hand lifted to her swollen cheek. "It is nothing, *patrón*." Her words came tumbling out in a rush. "The one they call Jole is a beast, but the old one stopped him. I am all right. The old one is very harsh, but he is not an animal. The one called Fane, he is an outlaw but a gentleman. Be careful, *patrón*. They are dangerous men. Except Arlo, the slow one, he is an innocent."

"This is almost over, Maria. Just a few more minutes."

"Be careful, *patrón*." She came and peeled Stitch out of his arms. She leaned against him and spoke in a whispered burst of words. "The old one wants to kill but Fane says no. Fane only wants money. Watch the old one, *patrón*." Ward gave her a quick nod and turned away.

When he stepped outside again, Fane called, "All right?"

Ward said, "Deal."

"Good. Let's get started. Put the gold down on

the ground right over yonder." He pointed to a spot in the center of the flat ground in front of the shack.

"You seen that gold yet, Fane?" Micajah wasn't above gloating, and his tone showed it.

"I seen it and I touched it and I got a sample in my pocket, Paw. Don't start trouble." He dug into his shirt and flipped a coin in the dirt in front of his father. "Chew on that if it'll make you feel better."

Micajah stepped forward and picked up the coin. When he raised his head again, he wore a broad smile. He rubbed the coin with his thumb for a moment before he slipped it into his pocket. "Now that's real money. None of that paper stuff weighs down a man's pocket like the real thing."

Pa waited, gaze fixed on Ward. At Ward's nod, he rode forward, dropped the bag, slowly turned his horse, and rode back to where he'd started. Ward walked Peepeye to join him.

Fane said, "You seem still a mite closer than I want you."

Ward answered, "Pistol range. That's what you said."

Fane narrowed his eyes, rode to stand over the gold, and squinted at Ward, gauging the distance. Finally, he nodded. "All right. Tell Maria to come out here, Paw."

Maria stepped through the doorway before Micajah could speak. She carried Stitch across the open space and stood beside the canvas bag.

"Arlo?"

"I'm coming, Fane. I done it. All the horses is ready." Arlo came from behind the shack leading the animals.

As soon as Micajah and Arlo were in the saddle, Fane passed his rifle to Micajah. "Now this here's the hard part. Ward, you and Mr. Baynes walk off a goodly distance and lay down your rifles. Paw and Arlo will ride off at the same time. You walk away from your rifles and Paw and Arlo keep on riding. If we do this right, nobody loses advantage."

Pa and Ward walked to the side, and Micajah and Arlo walked their horses away. By the time Ward and Pa laid aside their rifles and returned to their horses, Ward felt comfortable with the distance covered by Micajah and Arlo. They rode twisted in the saddle, both of them watching the scene behind them.

Fane picked up Stitch and perched him on a hip, cradled in his left arm. He stood with his foot on the reins of his own horse. "Now, Ward, bring your horses to me." He chuckled. "I'm going to hold the baby for a while. I'd feel mighty let down if you lost your good sense and tried to shoot me after we went to all this trouble."

Ward slid from the saddle. From the corner of his eye, he saw Pa do the same. Peepeye nuzzled Ward's chest, and he ran a hand down the velvet smooth muzzle. He stood for a moment, feeling like he was parting with half of himself.

"What's the holdup?"

Pa said bluntly, "Pet horse. Give him a minute."

Ward stripped off his saddle and saddlebags and dropped them to the ground. Pa busied himself doing the same thing with his horse. When both pack animals had been stripped, Ward walked to Fane, tied Peepeye's reins to his saddle, lined up Pa's horse and the packhorses, tied their reins so they'd lead properly, and then turned away.

"Just a minute." Fane spoke in a low tone. "Ain't that the same bay you had back in Louisiana? Ain't that your racehorse?"

Ward faced him. "Yeah."

"Well I'll be damned. I should've known him. Fancy that, after all these years."

"Yeah, fancy that."

"Ward."

"Yeah."

"I'm shamed about burning your house. I apologize for that."

Ward didn't trust himself to answer, so he stood silent.

"We plan to head for Mexico. Ain't no secret about it. Soon as I get so I don't have to watch my back trail no more, I'll make up a way to get that horse back to you, Ward."

"How do you think you'll do that?"

"Ain't got no idea, but I'll figure something out." Fane passed Stitch to Maria, picked up the bag of gold and mounted. He sat and waited for Ward to walk back to stand with his father.

Ward walked away. When he turned to stand beside Pa, Fane hadn't moved from beside Maria and Stitch.

Fane said, "This went off good because everybody did like he was told. This is the hardest part for you men. I know you'll be wanting to shoot at me while I ride off. Just remember, if I got to turn back and shoot, I'll be shooting at them." He pointed at Maria and Stitch. With that, he heeled his horse into a trot and rode toward Micajah and Arlo. They had stopped and were waiting for him on a low crest about five hundred yards away.

Maria picked up Stitch and ran toward Ward and his father. They trotted to meet her. As soon as she came up to them, she surrendered Stitch to Pa's open arms. Her first words came in the same rushed burst of words she'd used in the shack. "Rudi? Did Rudi die?"

Pa said quickly, "No, Maria, he was recovering in my house when we left Sacramento. He'll probably be up and walking around when we get home."

She crossed herself and sank to her knees. "Thank God."

Ward trotted to the rifles and brought them back. He handed Pa's weapon to him and stood with Nadine cradled in his arm. He stepped away from Pa and Maria to scan the surrounding hills, his head moving slowly back and forth.

"You looking for Luke and Cotton?" Pa asked.

"I can't figure it, Pa. They should have had

time to come up on us." He faced the barren, empty view and waved his free arm, a come-on signal. He turned to face a new direction and made the same signal.

"There!" Pa said sharply. "Look yonder." He pointed.

"That must be him." Ward repeated the signal and waited. In a few seconds, a mounted man came into sight, soon joined by another. Ward waited, shifting from one impatient foot to another, while the two horsemen approached. Sure enough, in a few minutes, he recognized Luke's massive figure. When they rode in, both horses showed heavy lather and stood with heads down.

Luke dismounted and said, "We tried to circle and ran into rough country, lost a lot of time, had to turn back and ride like hell. By then I felt we were so far behind we'd lose you unless we tracked you. I had to take it slow for fear they'd posted somebody to watch the back trail for us. I feared an ambush every minute. Is everything all right?"

"We got Stitch and Maria. That part is fine. I traded a bag of Pa's gold and Peepeye for them. I want both back." Ward walked to Luke's horse first, then to Cotton's, and finally to the pack animals. "I'm going to have to go to Mexico, but not today. These horses look beat."

"You sure you want to push this any further, Ward?" Luke's gentle question snapped Ward's head up, and he answered sharply.

"You think I wouldn't push anybody who stole Peepeye? You think I wouldn't push anybody who stole my Pa's gold?"

The sound of a distant shot rolled across the rocky land. Everyone went silent and turned toward the sound. Six or seven more shots tolled and echoed, spaced out seconds apart. They remained quiet, and after a few minutes, three more shots echoed, these coming close together.

Luke whispered, "How far?"

Pa held up a hand, still listening. After a moment, he whispered, "More than a mile I'd wager. What do you think, Ward?"

Ward stood and listened without answering. After about five minutes, he whispered, "I'm not a betting man, Pa. But if I wanted to wager, I'd like to bet Milton Baynes is out there taking pot-shots at Trampes."

Cotton asked, "What makes you think that's your brother, Ward?"

"That's his way. He always shows up when I have a need."

Cotton slanted a doubtful look toward Pa.

Pa nodded and said, "Milt was always a willful boy, given to riding alone, and always up to some kind of mischief." He smiled at Cotton. "If that was Milt, those might have been warning shots. Milt likes to stir the pot before he dips the ladle."

Luke chuckled. "Cotton, your mouth is hanging open. I told you my brothers are strange. For a lawyer, you're mighty forgetful."

# SEVENTEEN

Ward had to step away from the others. He couldn't get himself sorted out. His heart overflowed every time he looked at Stitch. He could already imagine Kit's face when he put the little fellow in her arms. He knew when she held Stitch and looked up at him, her eyes would melt his insides. Even though he'd prepare and plan to stand like iron, he'd dissolve, and she'd see, and she'd call him her cold gunfighter and laugh.

He could even conjure up the expression on Rudi's face when Maria sashayed into his view. The courtly horseman and the quiet little Maria would make a fine pair, and Ward suspected they had grown close to an agreement.

Everybody around the sorry little shack on a rocky slope near a dusty stage road wore big smiles. Cotton passed his secret bottle around, and even Maria tried a nip, although her face twisted into a knot at the taste of raw whiskey. Pa got out his pipe and settled himself comfortably with a smug expression, looking the perfect picture of the benign and satisfied grandfather.

Ward should be counting his blessings, and he did feel grateful, so much so that it nearly buckled his knees, but he had a gnawing black poison eating at his insides. He daren't let on. His own family would be aghast. Still, Ward alone suffered among the joyous. Normal people would regard him as a bizarre and twisted fool if they discovered that he grieved for a horse at a time like this. Yet, grieve he did, and he had to walk into the darkness to conceal the tracks of sorrow that ran down his cheeks.

Practical matters couldn't be ignored when a man had to provide for a family. Peepeye wasn't just a horse he'd treasured almost half his life. Peepeye was his show horse, the stud, the sire of a line of fine horses, the keystone in the structure of a stable of champions. A prudent man would never have risked such a valuable animal on a trip like this. But Peepeye was a trained gun horse, too, the deep well of power and skill and speed Ward dipped into when his spirit faltered.

Practical matters could break a strong man's heart. Ward tried to dodge, tried not to think about it, but the ugly truth kept nagging at him. He had no home. He had no money beyond pocket change, and he owed his father ten thousand dollars. Ward's mind whirled in circles when he tried to imagine how long he'd have to struggle to pay back such a monstrous debt. Payment would take all his earnings over absolute necessities. Every spare dime would go to paying the debt. His Kit would face years without the little extras her aristocratic background led her to take for granted.

The cold air seeped into him, and he stamped his feet to warm himself. After all these days of riding south, the world got colder instead of warmer. Ward walked over to his pack and unrolled his buffalo robe. He wanted to sleep with Stitch curled up beside him, but Maria would need the robe. He'd give it to her, and she'd expect to snuggle Stitch into it with her. She'd be scandalized if he demanded that Stitch sleep with him. It would insult her, imply that she wasn't up to what was her notion of woman's work. He should walk softly with this loyal woman. He remembered the sweet baby smell of his son in that tense first greeting in the shack. Maria had even managed to keep the little fellow clean.

Maria thanked him like he'd given her a handful of precious gems, her hands stroking the rough fur of the robe. He wandered to the fire and hovered for a while, listening to the quiet creep over the camp as everyone but Pa bedded down.

Pa always liked the first watch. Being a cautious man, he naturally assigned guards for their camp. Pa never considered letting down his defenses if enemies floated around the country, and they always did. If not prowling outlaws, then renegade Indians kept a man's wits sharp.

Cotton had protested when Pa assigned him no part of the night guard. Pa had just looked him in the eye and said, "You're a city man. Get your sleep. Listening to the night is a job for wild men." Cotton showed commendable cleverness. He shut up and went to sleep.

Ward approached his father with his blanket over his arm. Pa sat away from the light of the fire. No guard should ever sit outlined in the light, nor should he look at the fire. Standing in light and being blinded by it was only wise if a man had no enemies or had sentries posted like a military unit. Ward wrapped his blanket around himself just the way he liked it and sat down behind Pa, Nadine across his lap. He leaned against Pa's back and stared into the night. No need to speak. Pa felt no need either, so the night sounds came clearly.

Ward's eyes popped open. Something had wakened him. He blinked several times to clear the sleep from his eyes. The brim of his hat blocked his view, so he lolled his head back like a man moving in restless sleep. He kept his eyes moving. At night, if you stared at something, it faded away. In the dark, the smart man kept his eyes roving, never fixed his eyes for more than a second or two. Then it came again, and Ward knew this was what had wakened him. The hoot of a barn owl came softly.

"Well done, son." Pa's whisper came with an

almost silent chuckle. "I felt you wake when he called the first time."

Pa made a click with his tongue. The owl hooted twice. Pa clicked twice. Milt appeared like a ghost drifting on the wind. He reached out and tried to pinch Ward's nose and chuckled when Ward slapped his hand away. "Hey, Pa, little brother's awake."

Ward jumped to his feet and threw his arms around his brother. Pa rose and threw his arms around them both.

Milt's voice broke when he tried to speak, and he cleared his throat to try again. "I feared you were dead, Ward."

Ward drew back to look up into his taller brother's face. "What made you think that?"

"We'll talk later." Milt's whisper carried the laugh in it Ward had grown to love. Milt laughed at everything. "You got a whole tribe camped here?"

"We got a bunch," Pa said. "You hungry? We have food."

"Nah. Having too much fun to stop to eat." Milt's answer met Ward's expectation. Milt as much as said he was still on the war path. "What have you folks been up to, Pa?"

"Sit a spell, and I'll tell you about it."

"I need to go get my partner. Win's horse took a spill today. He's got no broken bones, but he's bruised from top to bottom, front and back. He thinks I'm trying to starve him to death, so he'll appreciate a bite or two, if you can spare it."

Ward asked, "Was that you doing the shooting we heard shortly before dark?"

"Might have been. Win and I did burn some powder. Had us a good chase for a while before he took a tumble. I nicked one of them, but I turned back to look after Win, so they got away. I'll be back in a minute or two." He slipped into the darkness like a liquid shadow.

Milt's minute or two turned into almost an hour. Pa sneaked around the camp, building up the fire and hustling food. He made no more noise than a field mouse, but Luke appeared beside him. Their heads came together, and Luke's hands rose briefly, fisted into a joyous victory sign. Pa had warned him of Milt's arrival. Luke's brief gesture matched a less reticent man's dance and shout of delight.

Luke met the slow-moving string of horses and lifted the slumped Win Mill from the saddle as effortlessly as he would a child. Ward kept his station while the others gathered around the fire, talking in such low tones he could hear none of it. Abruptly, Luke grabbed Milt's coat and shook him good while Pa drove a fist into his palm and looked up like he was giving thanks. Luke rose and dragged Milt to his feet. No, he did more than that, he nearly lifted Milt off his feet into the air. He spun Milt around and shoved him away from the fire toward Ward.

Milt walked slowly into the darkness and slumped down beside Ward. "Luke's mad at me."

"Luke? No, he must be joking. Luke never gets

mad. He's just like the rest of us. He's so glad to see you he can't sit still."

"He's not joking. He came close to popping me in the mouth."

"I don't believe it. What happened? What did you pull on him?"

"Well, I found something today, wandering around in the rocks and sand. Luke thought you might want to look at it. He suspicioned you'd think it important."

"What?"

"Come look, Pa said you could. He'll keep watch."

Milt rose and slipped through the darkness with his almost magic noiseless pace. He led Ward around the shack, past the corral, and into a clump of mesquite.

Ward gasped and froze. Peepeye stood hipshot, a feed bag covering his nose, chewing away and looking bored. Ward's knees wobbled under him when he rushed forward and threw his arms around the big bay's neck. Peepeye tossed his head in pretended irritation, lifting Ward's feet from the ground for a second, one of their oldest games. As soon as he came back to the ground, Ward began his habitual search for wounds or hurt places, running his hands all over the patient stallion.

Only after his inspection did Ward turn on his brother. "Why didn't you tell me you got him back, you son of a bitch? Now I know why Luke nearly popped you one. You wandered around and let me suffer all this time! How could you do that to me?"

"Easy. Little brothers got to learn to look after their own toys. When are you going to grow up? You need to be taught a lesson."

Milt, able to see in the night like an owl, moved his head just an inch or two, but it was enough. Ward's fist missed. Ward found himself wrapped in long arms squeezing him so hard his breath came out of him in a muffled groan. Milt eased off the pressure and whispered, "I saw a Trampe leading Peepeye, and I lost control. I went to shooting too quick. Lost my head. Win Mill spent two hours cursing at me, called me every degenerate and obscene name ever devised. He'll never let me live it down. I couldn't figure how anybody could get that horse from you without killing you. I thought you were dead, Ward. It's hard trying to shoot and bawl at the same time. Worst shooting I ever did in my whole life."

Ward wriggled and Milt released him, but Ward didn't step away from his brother. He stood close with a fistful of leather vest in his hand. Milt lowered his head to whisper close to Ward's ear.

"When I came to the camp, I didn't know what I'd find. When I sneaked up and took my first look, I saw Pa and Luke, but I didn't see you. I separated Peepeye from the other horses and put him out here, thinking Pa's heart would break seeing him so soon after losing you. When

I came close again, and I saw you with Pa and still alive, it dropped me like a shot. When I finished thanking the Lord and got up off my knees, I figured He'd forgive me if I made you wait a little while. I calculated you'd appreciate getting your pet horse back all the more with a little delay."

"Milt, I can never thank you enough for this. No way can I ever. I'm sorry I took a cut at you."

The smug whisper came with Milt's own brand of insult. "I know. Little brothers can't fight worth two cents, and they just keep soaking up favors. Big brothers learn not to expect anything from them."

"How did you get Peepeye from Trampe?"

"Shot him and chased him. He finally saw I was sincere after I chased him for quite a spell. Pulling that string of horses slowed him down, so he cut them loose. Lucky he didn't know my horse was worn down to wobbles and staggers. That's why it took me such a long time to get here. I walked all the way, so I couldn't get here before dark."

"You shot him?"

"Yeah, but not a good center shot, Ward. Like I said, I let myself get disturbed. That always makes for poor marksmanship. I knocked him sideways, but I didn't get him out of the saddle."

Ward untied Peepeye and started toward the corral. Milt trailed along.

"Ward, if you put that damn stud in the corral with the other horses and he kicks one of mine,

I'll whip your butt. I swear I will."

"Pick on somebody your own size. Which Trampe did you hit?"

"Fane. I got close enough to see him plain."

"Did you see the other two?"

"Yeah, for all the good it did me. Like I said, this wasn't a proud shooting day for me. Win never even got off a shot. All he did was a grand, flying flop when his horse fell out from under him. Wait!"

Ward stopped in alarm and reached for Jesse. He went into a crouch and searched for whatever had drawn the exclamation from his brother.

Milt's hand dropped on his shoulder. "Didn't mean to scare you. I just had a great idea."

"For heaven's sake, Milt."

"Great ideas come seldom. It just came on me out of the dark. I thought of how I can shut Win up. He peeled the hide off me about my poor shooting today." He snickered. "I been calling him dwarf. I'm going to start calling him tumbler. That'll shut him up." Milt snickered again, "You can't let a redhead get anything on you, Ward. They're vicious. I know what I'm talking about. I married one."

"Fane got away with ten thousand dollars of Pa's money, Milt."

"Is that all?"

"What are you talking about. That's a fortune."

"I got to take a closer look at my little nephew. I know he's liable to grow up to be a runt like you, but he ought to be worth more than that."

"May not seem like much to you. You don't owe it to Pa."

"Nothing to worry about."

"Not for you. It is for me."

"Your problem isn't ten thousand dollars, Ward. Your difficulty is you give up too easy."

"What? Who said anything about giving up?"

"You did. You just said Fane got away with ten thousand dollars of Pa's money, didn't you?"

"Yeah. I did. That's the truth."

Milt came out with his nasty snicker. "Not so. Now then, if I'd wanted to tell you the situation, I wouldn't have said that at all. I'd have been truthful with my big brother."

"What would you have said?"

"Me, now, I would have said Fane's got a head start with some of Pa's money. I wouldn't lie to you like you did to me."

"You think we can catch him, Milt?"

"I got to, Ward. I'm not like you. I'm a proud man. I care about what people think of me. I can't have Fane talking around about what a poor shot I am. I got to show him I can do better."

"Did Pa tell you about the blind eagles?"

"Nope. What's a blind eagle?"

"Go ask him. And bring me my blanket, will you? I think I'll sleep with this pretty horse."

# EIGHTEEN

Near Vallecito Stage Station, California
November 19, 1870

Ward awoke early that morning and walked softly to the fire to sneak a cup of coffee before the camp awakened. The first thing he saw was Stitch's tousled little head tucked under Pa's chin, both of them smiling in their sleep, wrapped in Pa's blankets. He stood for a minute or two, wishing he had an artist's skill. That would make a painting to touch the hardest heart.

Envy touched him. Pa could charm the arms off a brass monkey. He'd probably conjured up just the right words and made Maria feel like a queen granting a request. Pa could talk women's mysterious language. Ward knew he didn't have the knack and suspected he never would. If he'd asked to sleep with his own son, Maria would probably have gone into a snit, and he'd have felt like an ogre. So he slept with his horse.

Ward turned away shaking his head. Maybe when his hair started to show gray streaks, he'd learn the trick. For heaven's sake, he spoke three languages without stumbling, but he couldn't even persuade his wife's maid to let him tend to his own son overnight. Pitiful.

The camp stirred into activity as if a magic inner clock had tolled everyone awake at the same time. The friendly, lighthearted bustle seemed more like a social cookout than a group drawn together for serious purposes. That attitude changed instantly when Pa called for the men to gather, time for business.

The conference had rough spots. The need for speed pressed on everyone, and that made for blunt speech. Even so, it seemed to Ward they found common ground quickly and reached an agreement everyone could live with and not suffer hard feelings.

Win, so sore he could hardly move, agreed readily enough to stay behind and escort Maria and Stitch back home. The redhead's face was gray with pain, and he could hardly move a finger without grimacing. Until he had time to recover, a hard ride would be pure agony.

Cotton didn't convince so easily. He wanted to join the chase. Luke finally broke his resistance by making a request. Luke asked Cotton to help Win escort Maria and Stitch. With Win off his feet and hurting so bad, he'd need help. If Cotton didn't do this favor for him, Luke would have to take on that job. That would mean he couldn't ride with his father and brothers.

Luke's expression would have done credit to a child hearing a rumor there would be no Christmas this year. Cotton collapsed and said he'd be honored to do escort duty, though his silent stare called Luke vile names.

After the division of horses and supplies and the good-byes, the Baynes clan found themselves trotting through a bright midmorning sun. Pa, now clearly in command, said simply, "Milt will lead us where he last saw the Trampes. We'll look at tracks."

Nothing more was said for half an hour. Pa abruptly reined his horse to a stop and motioned to his sons to join him. "Time for plain talk. Just us. Just family."

He eased his horse into a walk, and his sons lined up on both sides of him. "The Trampes have my money." Ward leaned forward to speak, but Pa's stern glance and uplifted hand silenced him. "The money was mine when we started, it passed from my hand to Fane Trampe under duress, and it's still mine."

Pa's expression settled in rigid lines, and he stared straight at Ward. "Nobody asked me to lend him money, and I never offered it as a loan. If the money's lost, it's my loss. I risked that money to get my grandson back. My money. My risk. Understood?"

Ward settled back in the saddle. Pa's tone didn't invite discussion. He had truth on his side. Fact was, Ward never had a chance to ask for a loan. Pa just came up with the money. Ward had made it a loan in his own mind, and he still felt that way. Just because he didn't ask right out didn't change anything. Just because Ward felt positive his Pa would always stand behind him without him having to ask didn't make this deal less of a loan. But Pa was using his command voice. When he used that tone, further talk fell flat. His decision was made.

After a brief pause to let the challenge sink in, Pa went on. "I'm starting this ride with three fine sons. I may come back from this ride with three sons and a bag of gold. That'll be fine. I may come back with three sons and no bag of gold. I can live with that. What I don't want to do is come back from this ride without all three of my sons. Understood?" His glance settled on Luke and held.

Luke said, "Yes, sir."

Milt said, "Yes, sir."

Ward nodded reluctantly.

Pa leaned forward in the saddle and fixed his eyes on Ward. "I didn't hear you."

Ward said, "Yes, sir."

"Nobody takes long chances."

The chorus of "Yes, sirs" came quickly.

"Good." Pa broke into a wide smile and settled back in the saddle. "Boys, I'm feeling mighty good. I was about to compose myself and try to be content with an old man's memories. I thought I had to give up the idea I'd ever ride with my sons again. I feel ten years younger. This is worth ten thousand dollars to me. You boys ever see a finer morning?"

Milt eased ahead, leading the way, and Ward pressed Peepeye to keep pace. As soon as they drew beyond earshot, Ward said, "Pa's in an overbearing mood this morning."

Milt answered with an edge of irritation in his voice. "I hope you're satisfied, runt."

"Me? What did I do?"

"You brought that on all by yourself. Luke and I had to sit there and take a chewing you brought on. Pa uses that tone of voice on us about once every ten years. I ought to bust you one."

"Why me? I didn't do a blessed thing."

"No, not you. You just moped around camp like a snakebit puppy, tail between your legs."

"I never."

"Moping around about that money. What a crybaby."

"I never. Wait a minute. I never said a word about that money to anybody but you. Did you tell Pa?"

"Sure did."

"You son of a bitch."

"He asked me. I had no choice."

"You did so have a choice. You could have made one of your silly jokes or something. You could've dodged."

"Oh yeah? You think I'm going to look him in the eye and lie? You up to that, little brother? He said you looked worried rather than happy and did I know what was bothering you. Now, you tell me how to dodge that, smarty runt."

They rode for five minutes without exchanging a word. Milt said, "You figured it out yet? A dodge is the same as a lie. Anytime you deliberately hide the truth, that's lying. You go ask Luke. He's a lawyer."

Ward snickered. "That's what lawyers do."

"That's right, but they don't kid themselves about what they're doing. You go ask Luke."

"I didn't say I wanted you to lie."

"No. You just called me a son of a bitch for telling the truth."

"It wasn't just because of that. I didn't even need that. I have plenty of other good reasons."

Milt whipped off his hat and swatted Ward. Ward's hat fell to the ground, and he had to dismount to retrieve it. By the time he got himself back in the saddle, Milt was a hundred yards ahead.

Ward rode with a smile fixed on his face. It seemed like he and Milt had never been separated. Ward wondered what it would take to talk his brother into moving to California. That didn't sound easy. Then he speculated about what it would take to talk Kit into moving to Texas. They needed to build a new house anyway. Why not build it in Texas?

Not another living soul in the world could match Milt at deflating somebody who got a bloated idea of his own self-importance. When a man's pride pocket got overfull, Milt had the skill of a professional pickpocket.

Milt found the trail while still on horseback, but he soon dismounted and walked bent over so far his head looked lower than his knees. Luke, Pa, and Ward posted themselves on Milt's flanks and rear. They guarded him from three sides, while Milt knew he had to guard his own front. It had to be that way else the guard in front might muddle the tracks. Teamwork like this required no talk. It sprang from years of habit.

Milt snapped his fingers and pointed at Luke. Luke rode to him at once and dismounted. Milt pointed and Luke knelt to look closely at the ground. Milt moved several steps and pointed again, and Luke went through the same close inspection. Milt turned and pointed at Pa. They went through the same procedure. When Pa stepped up into the saddle, Ward came to Milt's side without needing to be waved in.

"Five horses. See here. Good tracks for one of them. Over here, see, clear tracks for the second. Now look here, see? That's the third one. Now you got to look real close, right along these rocks, see? Fane left some blood. See those spots? I didn't get him down, but I hit him."

Ward said, "Turned in front hooves on one of them. Two nails bent on the shoe of the right rear hoof of another. You see anything to help identify the others?"

"Yeah, look at the right front track on this one, Ward. That's a brand new shoe."

"I can't tell."

"Come over here. Better track. See?"

"Good eye, Milt. I see it now."

"Pa said Fane told you he was heading for Mexico."

"That he did."

"All right. I calculate we'll save time by looking for a fake run to the south. I don't remember Fane being stupid. He most likely told us he wouldn't head that way when he mentioned Mexico. We'll ride alert for a sudden turn."

"Likely."

"I suggested to Pa that we jump trail. He agreed and rode ahead."

"Good work." Ward mounted again and looked for Pa. He had already ridden about three hundred yards ahead. Pa stopped his horse, dismounted, looked at the ground, and pointed. Luke galloped ahead in the direction Pa indicated. Jump trailing went on in that manner all day. One man would ride ahead at a gallop, find tracks, and point the direction. The next would dash ahead in the indicated direction and do the same. Jump trailing allowed them to follow the tracks at a brutal pace, and the horses soon were well lathered even in the chilled weather.

Milt's guess proved correct about five miles south of the stage road when the tracks abruptly turned east. Expecting a turn, the trackers didn't even lose five minutes. Then the trail angled back to the northeast until it joined the stage road headed east. Pa found a campsite and called a halt in the failing light of evening.

"Looks more like he's heading toward Yuma than Mexico." Pa stood holding his saddle while his mount rolled in the dirt.

Milt said, "Seems like they'd split up or do something to make it harder for us. Maybe he doesn't think we're following. You don't suppose he figures to flat outrun us?"

Ward ran his hands over Peepeye and lifted each hoof in turn to be sure his stallion came through a hard ride over rocky ground without harm. Peepeye never passed a day in his life that Ward hadn't checked every inch of him. "Do you think Fane recognized you, Milt?"

"Unlikely. He didn't see me at all at first. The first notion he had that he was in trouble came when my bullet hit him. Micajah and Arlo were way up ahead of him. He had no real chance to look at me except quick glances over his shoulder while I chased him, and I never got very close. My horse just wasn't up to much of a run. Besides, Fane was hurting, I imagine. Most men find getting hit by a bullet bothersome. He rode like he was having trouble staying in the saddle, and he never got off a shot."

Ward stood idly rubbing Peepeye's rump. "But you got close enough to know who he was. He can see just as well as you."

"Binoculars, Ward. I had the advantage. I own a fine pair of stolen binoculars, courtesy of a store owner who helped a bunch of upstanding citizens of Goliad beat me up one time. Besides, I knew who I was looking for, having talked to one of the Trampe family and having been present when he committed suicide."

"Suicide?"

"Why certainly. He tried to shoot me. Best way I know for a man to shorten his life."

Pa said, "If Luke cooks, we'll have to eat fried corn meal again."

Milt and Ward answered in unison, "Luke cooks." Luke's fried corn meal patties with chopped peppers couldn't be matched anywhere.

Silent as usual, Luke smiled and started preparations.

Ward spoke in the tone of a man thinking aloud. "Fane didn't know about Luke and Cotton. With their packhorses, that makes four horses he doesn't know we have. He doesn't know who shot at him, so he doesn't know we got our horses back. That's four more horses he doesn't know we have. Do you suppose he's thinking that some stranger decided to shoot at him, just for the hell of it?"

Milt turned to look at Luke. "Where are you going to get grease to fry corn meal?"

Pa said, "You pester the cook, you get the job. You want to cook?"

"Never mind, Luke."

Pa said, "I think they're riding to Yuma as fast as they can. I think they need a doctor, and they need one badly. Micajah has one son who's worth a flip in his eyes, and he's wounded. That's the whole of it. He figures to get Fane patched up, and then he plans to outrun us."

Luke said softly, "They have doctors in Mexico, Pa."

Pa said, "Not as far as he's concerned. Micajah's a bigot. He figures anyone who doesn't speak English is a pagan or a papist. Any doctor who only speaks Spanish is probably eager to make a good Christian sicker. Nowhere on this trail are we more than half a day's ride from Mexico. He can always turn south again later if we start stepping on his heels."

# NINETEEN

APPROACHING YUMA, ARIZONA TERRITORY
NOVEMBER 21, 1870

The north wind turned sharp, carrying sleet, and the trail blurred just enough to cause doubt. The blowing sand, dust, and light sleet first softened outlines, then left just enough mark to detect anonymous tracks, then smudged out the trail entirely for short stretches. Ward had read only softened outlines for the last hour; he knew he was following somebody, but he doubted he was still on the right trail. Doubt when tracking creates slow work. Ward only hoped Milt's sharper eye didn't fail him, but Milt called a halt and spoke loud so all could hear over the wind.

"If they had been kind enough to stay away from the stage road, we'd have an easier time. The last few miles turned this into something more like guesswork than real trailing."

Ward rose from his hands and knees where he had been blowing hard to try to clear a track.

Pa said, "I've been spending more time watching the sides of the road than the trail. I think we'd have seen clear tracks if they turned off. I don't believe we'd have missed it. I'm pretty sure we're still headed in the same direction they are."

Ward asked, "Can anybody tell if we're gaining? I can't tell."

Pa answered. "Like Milt says, we're doing more guessing than anything else. This wind sure burns a man's eyes, doesn't it boys? I say we take a gamble. It looks to me like they're headed straight to Yuma. If they ride into a place where lots of people are running around, we'll have a hard time picking up the trail again. That may be their plan."

"How far to Yuma?" Ward asked, glancing around at the others.

Milt said, "I'd say about ten miles. We can make it before dark." He sent an inquiring look toward Luke.

Luke said something, but the wind whipped his comment away.

"What's that, Luke?" Milt leaned forward in the saddle to hear better.

Luke raised his voice. "Nine and a half."

Milt frowned in puzzlement. "Nine and a half what?"

"Miles to Yuma." Luke grinned.

"Yuk, yuk. Poor Luke tried to make a joke. So, maybe I'm a half of a mile off. Nobody's perfect." Milt's sardonic grin spread.

Luke shrugged. "You're just not cultured

enough to appreciate a clever man's wit. Win would catch the jest right away. He said that was about how far you missed with your shooting the other day."

Milt flinched, his grin vanished, and he pretended to slump in shame. "Damned redheads blab out every blasted thing they know."

Ward felt relieved when Pa gave his opinion of the conversation by kicking his horse into a brisk canter. Sitting out in the open chatting and chuckling in a piercing north wind didn't suit Ward either. Later, when Pa slowed again to a walk, Luke rode up beside Ward and extended a closed fist. Responding to the mute invitation, Ward stuck out a hand below the fist, and Luke dropped a deputy U.S. marshal badge into his palm. "I'm giving one to everybody. Stick it in your pocket. Those might come in handy but not if they're all in my pocket."

The lead-colored sky darkened early, and Ward felt he'd been delivered from evil when the ferry touched the bank on the Arizona Territory side. Boats made him feel helpless and queasy, and the solid ground under his feet came none too soon for his jumpy insides. The first livery stable they came to in Yuma already had a lantern lit in the tiny office when they pulled up in front.

Pa said, "Even if we find out something here and decide to ride on, let's get these horses a decent feed and get them out of the wind for a while. They're looking used up."

Ward joined Milt in a walk through the dim stable. "Think you might recognize their horses?" Ward asked in a whisper.

Milt shook his head. "I'm looking to see if one of them might jog my memory. You know how you only remember a horse sometimes when you see it again?"

Ward nodded, and they walked down the line, inspecting every horse. When they came back to the front, Pa shook his head to stop talk and led them out to the street. Then he said quietly, "I asked the hostler if anybody had passed a double eagle to him yesterday or today. He said no, but it was a good idea, and he'd be pleased to take on some of the strain if I had too many weighing me down." Pa flashed his grin with the corners pulled down. "Everybody's so burdened down with funny remarks today they have to spill the overload on me."

"I like this better than when we came through before, Pa. Remember? It was summertime then. Driest place in the world. You could pour water from your canteen and it'd never reach the ground. No eggs ever hatch here. They cook before the hen that lays them can cackle."

"Hush, Milt." Pa sounded like he had about taken his full load of jokes today. "Boys, Micajah Trampe used to be a man who enjoyed his whiskey. Unless he's reformed, he'll not be passing a saloon without having a taste. Even if they kept riding, he might have brought himself a bottle on the way through. Let's look around.

We'll ask if anybody's passed a double eagle across the bar."

Pa glanced at Ward and pointed at the left side of the main street. Ward and Milt always worked together, and Pa and Luke made another team. The four Baynes men separated without further conversation, Pa and Luke headed down the right side of the street. The unspoken plan demanded that they check any place where a man might spend money. Ward always walked inside while Milt paused at the door or stayed on the street. Mill didn't much like to go inside buildings, so he naturally didn't find comfort in towns at all.

Pa and Luke usually walked into places separately also. Pa said it bothered those who planned trouble to have to pay attention in two directions at once. Folks sometimes caught on that Pa and Luke were together because of the strong family resemblance. They looked more like brothers than father and son. Ward and Milt could pass as complete strangers to each other.

The first business Ward entered was a small adobe cantina. Strings of red peppers ran across the ceiling behind the bar, and the smell of tortillas and beans came stronger than the odor of tequila and beer. A strongly built Mexican bartender nodded. Ward greeted him in Spanish, and the bartender immediately broke out a wide smile.

Ward asked, "Has a stranger passed a double eagle to you in the last couple of days?"

The smile grew wider. "I could not give him change if he did, *señor*. Not unless he stayed and drank for a couple of days. This is not a place for rich men."

Ward thanked him and almost turned to leave when the man added, "The only double eagle I've seen all month was from the hand of the doctor. He was in here earlier today. He is a good man, but he has a big thirst. I give him a little credit, and he always pays sooner or later."

"May I see it?"

"Why, *señor*?"

"I search for double eagles made in 1870 without an eye."

Curiosity written all over his face, the bartender pulled his cash box from under the bar and extracted a shining gold coin. He inspected it and said, "It is an 1870 and the eagle has no eye. Who would notice such a small thing? Is it a fake?"

Ward extended his hand in invitation and the bartender handed the coin to him. He needed only a glance. He returned the coin and asked, "Where does the doctor live?"

"I do not want to bring trouble to him, *señor*."

"You will not. I just want to ask who gave him the coin."

The bartender paused, and his eye flickered to the scar on Ward's cheek. Ward could almost read the man's mind. The scar looked like a gun crease, a fighting man's wound, but this little Anglo didn't look dangerous. Besides, he spoke easy, polite Spanish like a grandee, and his coat came from an expensive tailor. Still, the man hesitated. Ward slipped his hand into his coat pocket and displayed the badge.

Ward continued to speak in formal Spanish, careful with legal words he seldom used, knowing that he risked sounding like a pompous ass. "I seek men guilty of arson, attempted murder, and extortion. You don't want to hold back information. I do not want to come back for you. If you do not tell me what you know, you will be helping them. It would be bad for you if I should learn of it. That would make me come back and cause you serious trouble."

The bartender leaned forward and glanced around as if he needed to reassure himself that the place was completely empty except for two of them. "The doctor says he has a man in his house, badly wounded, almost surely dying. There are two other men with the hurt one. You will be careful, *señor?* I don't want the doctor hurt. He is a good friend."

Ward nodded. "In this line of work, I am always careful. Where does he live?"

"His house is down close to the river. If you came across on the ferry, his house is the first one you would see off to the left. It is adobe, painted white, and it has willow trees all around it."

Ward slid a dollar on the bar and met the man's eye. "Thank you. Buy yourself a drink. You have done a good thing today." He glanced back when he reached the door. The bartender stared at the coin, still undecided about whether to pick it up. Ward smiled acknowledgment of the man's dilemma. When a man couldn't yet decide whether he'd done the right thing, he'd best be careful about accepting payment for what he'd done. It could be bad luck. Ward had grown up with people who shared the same superstition. Payment for evil or disloyal deeds risked the Judas curse.

As soon as he stepped outside, he gave the clenched fist success signal to Milt. Milt slouched closer, the picture of a bored idler. "First place you walked into, for heaven's sake. You find out something already?"

"Wounded man at the doctor's house. Remember that white house down by the ferry? The doctor paid the bartender with a blind eagle."

"It's about time we had some good luck. Let's get moving while we still have a little light left."

"You want to go down and watch that house, Milt? I'll go get Pa and Luke."

Milt said, "I wish we had time to get the horses. I'll be sore if they jump in the saddle and ride away from us.

"I didn't see any horses near the house. You going?"

Milt turned without answering and idly wandered toward the river, looking like he had to keep walking to avoid falling asleep.

Ward waited until Luke came out of an adobe

building across the street. Luke's gaze slid across Ward without sign of recognition, but Ward saw his head give a slight jerk when he saw the fisted success signal. He wandered across the street and came up to Ward, gesturing with a questioning wave of his arm down the street like a man asking directions. Ward spoke quickly.

"Doctor passed a blind eagle. Has a wounded man in the white house down close to the ferry. Milt's already going that way. If I know him, Milt will surely be behind the house checking to see if they have horses held close by."

Luke gave a little nod and wave as if saying thank you for directions. "You take the front. Pa and I will take the sides." He headed back across the street.

They made the trip widely separated. No casual onlooker would see a group of men moving toward a common destination. Ward had a confused moment when he neared the house. The doctor had built it facing the river rather than the road. Which side would be called the front? He hesitated to let Pa and Luke select their positions, and he ended up with the side of the house that faced the road.

Pa ended up in front, Luke in back, Ward on one side, and Milt on the other. No doors or windows showed on Ward's side, so he moved to join Luke. When he got close, Luke wagged his hand back and forth, indicating no doors or windows at the back either. He pointed at Ward, then toward Milt's side. Ward slipped through the deepening darkness toward Milt, knowing Luke would move to join Pa.

Ward felt a growing sense of satisfaction. No sense in any Baynes clansman guarding a blank wall. Evidently, the doctor's house had only a front and a side door. That allowed the usual teamwork to come into play, with two Baynes men on each side, and none of them would have to stand alone to face two or three Trampes at once.

Trotting horses came down the road and pulled around the house toward the river side. Ward shifted to see what was happening, motioning to Milt to stay put. Ward changed his position just in time to see a tall, lanky figure riding at the head of four led horses pull up and hurriedly slide to the ground. The figure had already taken four or five steps toward the house when Pa stepped into view and shouted, "Stop right there, Micajah."

Micajah never broke stride, but his rifle whipped up toward Pa with the incredible speed of the seasoned Louisiana sharpshooter. From the shadows, Luke's rifle boomed. The blossom of flame from the muzzle flashed light through the semidarkness like a bolt of lightning. Micajah's rifle cracked a split second later, but flame from the weapon spurted skyward when his tall frame arched backward from the strike of Luke's bullet.

Micajah's rifle fell to the hard soil with a clatter and he staggered back a couple of steps. Then he recovered his balance and straightened to his full height. "That wasn't you, Darnell. Who shot me?"

Luke cranked another shell into his Spencer, and Micajah's head swung toward the distinctive noise. "That was me, Mr. Trampe. I'm Luke Baynes. I couldn't stand here and let you shoot my Pa. I'm sorry, sir, but I had no time to give you fair warning."

"By God, Darnell . . ." Micajah Trampe's voice broke, and he almost fell backward, but he shifted his feet, caught himself, and stood again like a soldier at attention. This time the groan of effort it took him came plainly, and his voice had some of the groan still in it when he spoke. "By God, Darnell, I'll say one thing for you. You taught your sons to be polite." Slowly his body began to buckle forward. His voice came thin and strained, hardly above a murmur. "Spoken like a man, Luke." He tried to take a step forward to catch his balance again, but his knees buckled, and he fell as if every joint gave way at once.

Ward walked closer, knowing Milt would guard his back and watch the door on that side of the building. Pa stepped to Micajah's side, big hands extended and ready in case Trampe tried to put a knife or pistol into play. With Jesse now drawn and ready, Ward felt no alarm. When Pa got close enough to get his hands on a man, nobody with Trampe's slim build would ever do him harm.

Pa's voice came gentle when he asked, "How bad are you hit, Micajah?"

"Dead center, Darnell. Don't concern yourself. Nothing you can do."

"This is the way it had to end, Micajah."

"I know. I knew it the first night after we burned that boy's house and took away his baby. I lost my Bible that very night. It was a sign, but I didn't pay no heed to it."

"You need anything?"

"I got a bottle on that horse yonder. Let that boy Luke get it for me. He's a good boy. He can get your gold too. It's with the bottle." Luke trotted to the cluster of horses only a few feet away and fumbled frantically with the saddlebags.

Micajah mumbled something and Pa leaned forward to hear him. Pa said, "I will, Micajah."

Luke came back with the bottle after hardly fifteen seconds had passed and jerked out the cork with the distinctive squeak that waters the mouth of every drinking man. When Luke knelt and extended the bottle toward Micajah, Pa said quietly, "Never mind, Luke. He couldn't wait."

Luke knelt with the bottle extended toward Micajah for a long time, as if Micajah might still reach for it if it were offered patiently enough. Finally, his arm dropped slowly, and he pushed the cork back in. "I wish the Lord would have let him have a last drink, Pa. That wasn't much to wish for."

Ward asked, "Did he say something to you, Pa?"

"Yes, he did, son." Pa came to his feet, blew out a long breath, and lifted his face to the sky. "He said, 'Pray for me, Darnell,' and I told him I would."

"Is it finished, Pa?" Luke asked.

Pa stood staring at the sky for several seconds without answering.

Ward said, "Not for me, Luke. There are still two more Trampes. I think both of them are in this house right here, and they're both too rotten cowardly to even open the door to see if they can help their old man."

Pa said, "Ward, your son may be almost home by now. My gold, or most of it anyhow, is in Luke's hand. Isn't that enough, son?"

"No, sir, not for me. A fine man who works for me still lies in pain from his wounds if he lives. My house and barn lie in ashes. My wife's hair may be white from worrying by now."

Pa hesitated. "Well . . ."

The night had taken away the light, and Milt's voice seemed that of a spirit from the darkness. "I'm with Ward. A job started should be finished."

Luke asked, "Is that righteous? What's left but pure vengeance?"

Milt answered quickly in a low tone that carried so well it seemed that he stood beside them in the dark. "I admire purity. If I hadn't stayed in Goliad purely for vengeance, I'd have never tarried there long enough to win the purest wife a man ever met."

251

Pa chuckled. "I'm not sure it's fitting to be amused, but this is so strange it tickles my funny bone for some reason. I can't imagine four grown men standing over a dead body in a cold night wind arguing about whether or not it's time to stop killing."

Ward, having spoken his piece, found himself scanning the quiet darkness and wondering what kind of place Yuma must be. Two gunshots in the quiet of the evening hadn't attracted attention from anyone. But the evening hadn't been quiet. The song of the wind mixed with the nearby rush of the mighty Colorado River allowed no true calm at this spot.

Luke finally broke the silence that had seemingly held forever. "I'd not forgive myself if the Trampes came back on Ward later. They came at his family once already, searching for blood vengeance. It might happen again unless we finish it here."

Pa answered quickly, almost as if relieved. "Your play, Ward. How do you want to do it?"

"I want to go through that door and search that house. If I find a Trampe, I'll kill him. All I want from you is to watch to see nobody slips away from me."

"Elegant. Simple." Milt sounded smug.

"These Trampes are quick with guns, Ward, and you have to watch for Arlo. You made a promise. We're all bound by it now." Pa sounded the same as when he warned Ward that powder had to be kept dry on a hunting trip.

"If Arlo doesn't pick up a gun, my promise holds, Pa."

"How do you plan to get in the house," Luke asked.

Ward laughed. "I'm going to knock on the front door like a white man."

"Stand to the side like a smart man," Milt said in his disgusted tone. "Some smart people shoot through the door when white men come around."

"Enough talk." Ward walked to the door, stood well to the side, and tapped the panel with Jesse's barrel. The door opened quickly, and a small, rotund man wearing a white cotton coat stared at him.

"Step outside, doctor. I have business inside. No call for you to get hurt."

"Unless you intend to shoot a weak-minded boy or a dead man, you have no business in my house."

"A dead man?"

"Well, not at the moment, but he doesn't have long in my opinion. He's dying."

"I think I'll decide that, doctor."

He stepped aside and waved Ward inside. Ward slipped past him and pressed himself against the wall of a narrow hallway, Jesse moving back and forth in search. The doctor walked briskly past and said, "Come with me." The interior of the adobe house was so brightly lighted Ward had to narrow his eyes. The lack of windows had given no hint that a lamp would be lit in almost every corner inside the house.

He pulled aside a curtain at a doorway and Ward saw Fane lying on a bed. Arlo sat in a corner. Arlo jumped up and smiled. "Hello, Ward. Where's Stitch? You bring Stitch with you?"

Attention focused on Fane, Ward said, "No. How's Fane?"

"He's sleeping, Ward. He fell asleep and Paw had to tie him in the saddle. He won't wake up."

Jesse in hand, Ward edged closer. One more bullet and it would all be finished. Both Fane's hands lay on top of the blanket covering him. When Ward stepped closer, Jesse's barrel rock steady, Fane's eyes popped open and his lips worked. The silent appeal in his eyes caused Ward to bend closer.

"Look after Arlo." His voice came in the dry whisper of late falling leaves on a windless day.

Fane's eyes closed, but he opened them again with tremendous effort. In the face of his direct, agonized stare, Ward had no time to think. The words came from him unbidden. "I will, Fane. I will."

Ward straightened and the doctor spoke from the doorway. "Did he speak?"

"Yes, he did."

The doctor shoved Ward aside. Ward holstered Jesse and stepped over to stand beside Arlo. Holding Fane's wrist, the doctor stood with his watch in his other hand. "Did you hear what he said?"

"Yes, I did."

Lowering Fane's hand to the blanket, the doctor jerked his head toward the doorway. As soon as Ward cautiously backed out, the doctor said in a low tone, "I think you just heard that man's last words. I don't expect him to last through the night. What did you tell him you would do?"

"Never mind."

The doctor shrugged. "All right, but I think that was a dying man's last request. I heard you say you'd do something. I hope, for the sake of your conscience, you'll do what you promised."

"None of your damned business."

"Correct. What else can I do for you?"

"Is Arlo going to stay here with Fane tonight?"

"He can, if he wants. That old man said he'd be back with fresh horses. Was that what the shooting was all about?"

Ward ignored the question. "Have you been paid for looking after Fane?"

"Yes, generously."

"You say Fane's dying?"

"I think so."

"You been paid to bury him?"

"No."

"How much do you need to bury a man here? To bury him decently."

"Twenty dollars should do it."

"There's another dead one out in front."

"Then that'll take another twenty dollars."

"Wait. I'm coming back." Ward went outside. "Pa, I need forty dollars."

Pa motioned to Luke, and he dug into the

canvas bag for two of the blind eagles. He passed the coins to Ward. Back inside again, Ward handed the coins to the doctor, who accepted them without comment.

"Did you get anything to eat yet, Arlo?"

Arlo nodded, and Ward turned to the doctor. "I'm coming after him in the morning. Will you look after him till then?"

For the first time, the chubby little physician smiled. "I've got a bed for him, and I'll feed him a good breakfast." He extended a hand. "I'm Dr. Andrew Stone."

Ward accepted the handshake. "I'm Ward Baynes."

The doctor's eyes widened. "I think I've heard of you Mr. Baynes. Are you *the* Ward Baynes from Louisiana?"

"Yeah. Lots of people have heard of me."

Ward turned to Arlo. "Arlo, I'm coming after you in the morning. You'll be coming home with me."

Arlo smiled. "Will Stitch be there?"

"He sure will."

"I got to ask Paw."

"I think your Paw would be pleased, Arlo. Fane wants you to go with me too. That's what he told me just a minute ago."

"You sure it's all right, Ward?"

"Yeah. I need you to help me look after Stitch."

Arlo's head bobbed and his smile widened. "I can do that, Ward. I can do that."

Ward went outside again and explained to his family about Fane and his promise to look after Arlo.

They all stood in the freezing wind for a long moment of silence.

Luke asked, "You don't feel the need to shoot anybody, Ward? You past that, are you?"

"It's finished, Luke."

"Years ago, I thought you had too much hate in you. I told you then that you had to whip it. Maybe you won today. Maybe you finally got it whipped."

Pa said, "I guess I need to find a telegraph. I need to tell Mr. Pinkerton to call off his agents."

Milt said, "That's it then. The war's over. Let's go get something to eat. All of a sudden, I'm hungry."

# TWENTY

Ward sat in the saddle and looked at the pitiful little shack. Every time he came home to it, memories of the shocking blaze came back, with walls falling and sparks climbing to heaven. The memory of losing a home stays with a man for a long time. Maybe, when the rebuilding finished and they could move into their new home, the nightmare would recede.

Pa had a good time showing him the books and explaining how his part of the Baynes property amounted to quite a sum of money. Seems Ward Baynes wasn't nearly so broke as he'd thought. He'd started his ranch on his winnings from a horserace back in Montana, and he'd forgotten his share in the gold-mining venture. Pa had been investing his share and it had grown. Pa also mentioned, in passing, that Milt tried to give him a huge chunk of money to help Ward. Pa sent him back home with his money.

He rode to the shed to put Peepeye to bed, but Arlo came running to take the reins. Finger to his lips, he whispered, "Don't make no noise or Miss Kit'll fuss at you. Stitch is taking his nap. I'll take care of Peepeye. I can do that."

Ward dismounted and walked to the house, hardly believing he'd trust any other man in the world to look after Peepeye, especially a Trampe. He stepped inside, hung his hat and coat on a peg, and sat in his rocker without speaking. Kit smiled at him over her sewing. Stitch lay asleep in his little bed against the wall.

Ward whispered, "Can we talk?"

She answered in a normal tone. "You're home early. It's nice to see you in the middle of the afternoon for a change. Yes, we can talk. He's had a good nap. It won't hurt if he wakes."

"I want to talk about Arlo."

"All right. Have you found a place for him?"

"You've been patient. We've been home a month. I got to tell you, Kit. I haven't been looking."

"Oh?"

"I'd like him to stay with us. He's mighty useful. I know it's a burden to you to have a simple boy around, but I've come to have an affection for him. He loves Stitch. Thing is, we can't have him around unless you agree to it."

"Oh?"

"Now you're mad at me."

"Yes, I am. In fact, I'm furious."

Ward leaned forward and looked at the floor, elbows on his knees. "I figured you would be. I'm sorry. It's a dumb idea, but I can't seem to put it from my mind."

"How else do you expect me to feel when you're dishonest with me?"

Ward straightened. "Dishonest? I never."

"Oh?"

"When? What're you talking about, Kit?"

"You said him staying with us was just for a while till you could figure out what to do with him. You never planned any such thing. You wanted to keep Arlo with us from the start. You lied."

"Well, I thought you might be easier in your mind about what you decided if you got to know him a little. I thought you could help me figure out the best thing."

"Dishonest."

"All right. I was afraid you'd say no."

"You could have said you wanted to keep him around right at the start and put my mind at ease. Oh, no, you have to make everything hard for me."

"Kit, what are you talking about?"

"I've been afraid you might send him away, maybe to some awful place where people wouldn't understand him, where they might be mean to him."

"You mean you don't mind? I've got to where I depend on him. I'd miss him something terrible. But you got to agree, Kit. You know I couldn't do something like that unless you agreed to it. We always, both of us, got to agree on important things. I feel I've taken responsibility for him. I promised his dying brother. It's a thing that lies heavy on my mind."

Kit kept her gaze fixed on her sewing. "Hush, Ward, you're beginning to babble. No need to persuade me. Besides, I know all those things. Arlo stays. I knew I'd have to have patience with you, a man without a soul. No woman marries a cold, vicious gunfighter without knowing she'll have to have patience."

Ward jumped up and walked around the tiny room, rubbing his hands together. "You're a nice woman. I could fall in love with you, given a chance to hang around long enough."

She bent to her sewing basket. "Arlo went to town to get the mail today. The postmaster sent us a note along with our mail."

"We had mail? Good. Who from?"

"First, the postmaster's note." She handed it to Ward.

Ward took it and read aloud, "This man says he's Arlo Baynes, so I gave him your mail." Ward sat back down in his rocker. "He knows Arlo. Wonder why he sent that note."

Kit said, "It shows you, Ward. Even the postmaster knows him. He thought it would please us to know Arlo feels part of the family. Everybody likes Arlo."

"Who else wrote?"

"Your brother. Milt has a baby boy he spends

261

several detailed pages describing inch by inch. He also writes a couple of pages praising his wife, but not inch by inch, thank heaven. The other letter comes to me from Helen. You can't read it. It's private."

"Hand it over."

"No, it's mine."

"Hand it over."

"I'll tell you one thing, just one thing, but I'll never let you read it."

"All right, tell me one thing."

"You know how Luke has awful nightmares after having to kill someone?"

Ward stiffened. "Yeah. Luke suffers. I know."

"She says she has found a way to distract his mind when he awakens in the night."

Ward settled back in his rocker, puzzled, until he looked up at his wife's blooming complexion. She glanced at him, merely a flicker of her eyes, and said, "If you ever give her a hint I told you, I'll kill you, Ward Silvana Baynes. She'll die if she ever finds out I told. That's a confidence."

Ward rocked comfortably back and forth. "Maybe there's hope yet for that prissy Yankee woman.

# McCORD ON McCORD

My grandmother started life as Stella Cowan. The Cowans trace back to John Locke and his father, General Matthew Locke, and through Jane Rutherford to her father, General Griffith Rutherford. William Jones Cowan, my great-grandfather's uncle, joined Colonel James Walker Fannin's regiment, and his name appears on the monument with the others who lost their lives at the Goliad massacre. Benjamin Francis Cowan, my great-grandfather, was "furloughed" home after he spent three weeks in the "Gangrene Camp" from wounds inflicted by General Grant's artillery at Petersburg in 1864.

My great-grandfather on the McCord side, a Dallas millionaire early in this century, hired detectives to trace the McCord family tree. Told that an English ancestor was hanged for poaching in the king's forest, he dumped the enquiry, spent his money, and left his progeny to earn our daily bread. Our genetic poaching skills diluted by time and intermarriage with the less gifted,

McCords regressed to becoming engineers, architects, teachers, and mechanics. But the dubious heritage still persists — some of us practice law, and I write novels.

Handed a BB gun at age five and told to keep marauding sparrows from dining at our chicken troughs, my interest in weapons came alive, and I later took eagerly to competitive rifle matches and hunting.

Boyhood years as an amateur boxer, competing in three weight divisions as I grew, taught me that true defeat comes only to those who quit. Then twenty years as an infantry officer put me in close contact with the best men our country can produce.

To those critics who say Western heroes are too tall and wide to be believed, I say, "I've seen their real-life sons and daughters tested. When I write about their imaginary fathers and mothers in my fiction, why should I make them less worthy than their real, superb, living sons and daughters?"

The history of the American West draws me like none other. Books on this subject must be held just right, else romance and adventure pour out in your lap, soak through your chair, and drench the carpet. Mexicans fight Mexicans, Indians battle Indians, Irish railroaders dynamite rocks to fall on competing Chinese workers and the Chinese return the favor, white men feud, and everybody brawls with everybody in all kinds of weather on every type of terrain. The challenge of settling the West didn't appeal to weak or timid men and women, and its story doesn't seem credible to them now.

To mark human perversity, survivors often married their enemies' kinfolk, creating the most interesting and varied bloodlines on earth and the most fascinating and exciting people anywhere. To research and write a Western novel requires me to visit spectacular places, read spellbinding references, and talk to enthralling people. It's heavy work.